# BY SAMUEL YELLEN

# The Wedding Band

# The Wedding Band

## Samuel Yellen

NEW YORK

*Atheneum*

1961

*To my mother*

AND

*To the memory of my father*

# The
# Wedding
# Band

# *One*

When Mama died, I got her gold wedding band. Not that there was any unseemly squabble. After all, I *am* the eldest. And anyhow, and more to the point, what would Christina want with that plain, worn, outmoded broad yellow band faintly engraved on the inside in baroque flourishes

*MD to EH*

followed by a tuft of scratches where the date had been crudely scraped away? Poor foolish Mama, keeping up her pathetic concealments, pretensions, evasions, and mystifications to the very end! No, the unadorned fact, as we scholars are given to say, is that the band descended to me by default. Christina came for and carried off the diamond ring (two and a quarter carats) and diamond earrings (three quarters of a carat each) which Papa, in one of his grandiose moments, gave Mama on, or near, their twenty-fifth wedding anniversary. Older and unfortunately bigger though I am, I wouldn't care to, and probably couldn't, stand up to Christina when she is after something. She is not exactly the kind of woman who weeps over all the babies, little birds, and beautiful flowers in the world. Besides, as she always manages to remind me, I am an old-maid schoolteacher (thus she everlastingly depreciates the college professorship I took so long earning) with a perfectly adequate salary for my trifling needs and with no costly children to bring up. Well, I don't need Christina to tell me I'm a woman unwed, unwanted, unfulfilled. I didn't have the slightest intention of wrangling over those diamonds, and I really had no wish to possess them. As for Aldous, our baby brother, now forty years old—as I could have predicted, he didn't even come to the funeral.

Let Christina set me down for the impractical simpleton I very likely am. No doubt everything works out for the best in this best of possible worlds. No doubt, no doubt. Actually, I *wanted* the wedding band. It was the only authentic memento of Mama. It represented her the way the diamonds never could. In a sense, it was part of her, for she never took it off, and the pale gold had come to be embedded in the flesh of her finger like a discoloration of the skin. That was, of course, while Mama was still plump—nay, *obese*—before the illness of the last three years pared her down so that the band rattled around on her phalange. Even then, the undertaker must have had a time getting it off past the great crooked knuckle. Since Papa's huge bulk, thanks to the roulette wheel of the genes, devolved upon me, the band isn't loose on *my* finger. Risking the badinage of my sportive spinster colleagues, I wear it on my right hand. But often, when I should be reading blue books and term papers or turning over the marginal glossographical soil for another learned article on medieval literature, I have the band off my finger, rolling it fondly in my hand or studying the faded inscription.

*MD to EH*. Meyer Davidov to Eleanor Harper. Now that I think of it, I almost never heard Mama called Eleanor. (What dynes of agitation reside in that commonplace little ad-

verb "almost"!) It was generally "Mrs. Davidov." Or, on occasion, "Nell" to the few Jewish
friends who were finally able to overcome the
alienness of her being gentile. Papa called her
Nellie except when he happened to be bored
and ready for a bit of improvised melodrama.
Then it was "Old Lady." That never failed to
bring on the full flamboyant scene. Poor Mama
tripped no light fantastic. It was not only that
the eighteen long months when Bubbeh (Papa's
mother) interminably lived and interminably
died with us took all the gambado out of her.
Mama had, *ab ovo,* not a pinch of humor in her,
and Papa's sardonic Jewish banter always baffled
her. Besides which she was virulently sensitive
to being four years older than Papa, so that
"Old Lady" invariably succeeded in stirring up
the sleeping devils and bringing on a fine theatrical storm which would sputter for hours—
indeed, long after even Papa had wearied of the
game. How often that scene was played before
us children! It was like witnessing some ancient
extravagant ritual whose original purpose and
meaning have long been forgotten but whose
fixed procedure and formularies can still pro-

duce something like the original frenzy.

Usually the time would be early evening. The setting would be our cramped and shabby dining room, with the electric bulbs in the pendant rococo cut-glass chandelier glaring above the rectangular table where we were seated, I at Papa's right, Christina and Aldous at his left, Mama at the foot. The main part of the dinner would be over. Papa would already have asked us in turn what we had done during the day, all the while eating, noisily and with relish, the *gefillte* fish or the marinated herring, the soup with *kreplach* or *knaydlach* in it, the braised brisket or the *flaumen tsimmes,* the *kasha* or the potato *latkes,* the many thick slices of fresh warm rye bread shot through with caraway seeds and generously (as well as with an unorthodox disregard for the proper separation of *milchiges* and *flayshiges*) spread with butter, and all this accompanied by much mopping of the mouth with the napkin and much spattering of the white tablecloth in front of him. Papa was not a neat eater. Then before the compote of raisins, prunes and dried apricots, peaches, and pears had been dished out, he would push his dinner plate aside and, with a wicked smile on his big fleshy, swarthy, handsome Jewish face, would say, "Well, Old Lady, permit me to compliment you on a delicious *tsimmes*."

"Look who is calling me old."

"Yes, Old Lady! That's what I said. Old! Old! Old!"

With a forced little laugh, Mama would say, "And I suppose you think you're a young man."

"That's right, Old Lady. I still got plenty of life in me and I'm still a young man."

"That's what you say."

"No, that's what all the girls say. Ask Molly or Jenny or Billie or any of the girls at the Market. They'll be glad to testify I'm still a young man."

"Young man! Some young man! What you are is just a silly old goat," Mama would say ineffectually while Papa would guffaw until he ended up in an explosion of coughing. That would be the turning point. With us children looking on, frightened (except for Christina) and yet fascinated, in an instant the tone of the scene would darken as the underlying regions were touched where Mama had been brooding all day on her wrongs, both the very real and the fancied. "Meyer, how many times have I begged you to hold your napkin to your mouth when you cough at the table?"

"So now, Mrs. Emily Post, we're becoming all of a sudden elegant."

*"Es iz a shande fur die kinder* (It's a disgrace for the children)," Mama would say, turning to Yiddish with her settled and unshakable delusion that we children couldn't understand it. In actuality, not only could I understand it and speak it but Papa had even had me taught to read and write a little. And I must add that to hear Mama speak Yiddish in her flat Midwestern-gentile intonation always sounded bizarre to me. She lacked the Yiddish *nigen,* or melody.

Then as Papa's eyes blazed, she would turn back to English. "You don't have to behave like a filthy old man."

The furious blood would blacken Papa's face. And Mama would ostentatiously quit eating and set her plate to one side, as if Papa's table habits were simply too gross for her to bear. How much of this was genuine distaste, and how much a calculated piece of histrionics to get back at him, I never could be sure. Perhaps even Mama could not say. But Papa would pound the table with his enormous hairy fist so that the dishes jumped. And his deep, rough, rumbling voice would thunder, *"Ach, du alte macheshayfeh!* You old witch! What bad angel ever brought us together! And why, why, why did I ever marry you!"*

That's when Aldous would leave the table and go into Christina's and my bedroom and shut the door.

By their fruit shall you know them. But these are indeed strange fruit begotten of Meyer and Eleanor Davidov. And bearing strange names—Alexandra, Christina, Aldous. That was, of course, Mama building a levee to keep the Jewishness of Meyer Davidov from flooding over. Papa was not one to worry himself about the mystical powers of names. To him, I was simply Lexie, Christina was Teena, and Aldous was Zooneleh. Unless Papa happened to be hugging us to his great warm belly and kissing us juicily in one of his frequent displays of affection. Then we were indiscriminately and *con amore* "Sweetheart Sweetheart Sweetheart" or "Darling Darling Darling."

Yet how to explain or account for such strange and diverse fruit all from the selfsame parent stem? Predestination? Heredity? Fortune? Or perchance one of those newer binomial gods worshiped by our innocent present-day social scientists—Environmental Circumstance, Cultural Envelope, Statistical Probability, Genetic Factor, Childhood Trauma, Conditioned Reflex, Penis Envy, Toilet Training? As if these explained or accounted for, instead of merely supplying the inadequate wordage with which to try to talk about. How much more exciting (and at least as satisfactory and true) to summon up the quaint antique locutions of the medieval almagest! The zodiacal constellations wheeling about the celestial equator, the planets wandering fatefully in and out of the heavenly mansions, the greater and lesser evils and the greater and lesser fortunes raining down their influences, the correspondences between macrocosm and microcosm, the four elements, the four qualities, the four humours; to be born, as Alex-andra Davidov was, under Virgo, with hot chol-eric Mars in the House of Parents—for a whim-sical obscurantist spinster living alone with her thoughts, all this does suggest a little of the irony and the drama of our enigmatic lives.

Or perhaps it all turns on nomenclature, and our very names, as Mama was so supersti-tiously convinced, doom us. Poor foolish Mama, whose magpie head rattled with odd shards of popular misconception and misinformation picked up at random and tenaciously treasured. And yet, except for me, Mama did in a sense win out. Consider Christina. No one would take her for any part Jew. Even as a child she was, as Papa so often said, *a kalte shickse ohn a Yid-dishe neshomeh.* Yes, a cold, calculating gentile (female gender) utterly devoid of a tender and sensitive Jewish soul. Not one minim of Meyer Davidov's germ plasm made its way into Chris-tina. Physically she was a replica of what Mama must once have been—a good-looking darkling blonde, of medium height, slender but not boy-ish in figure, with an oval, well-boned face, reg-ular features, a fair, satiny skin brushed with tawny, and grayish-blue eyes. Even now, in her middle forties, she can wear a size-twelve dress and show off her slim, shapely legs, arms, and shoulders. Which she *does* find occasion to do. Ah, I'm afraid that there speaks the aloes of envy!

Nevertheless, setting aside the grievance of the ungainly ill-favored old maid, Christina *is* one of those women who dedicate themselves to the body beautiful. She is always meticulously turned out, overlaid with a hard-baked enamel like a professional model, her blond coiffure contoured as if cast in a mold, her fingernails lacquered in crimson, her breasts rigidly shaped and uplifted like an offering, her body elegantly girdled and sheathed, her legs shimmering in nylon, her imported Parisian shoes curving up extravagantly to the spike heels. In her lurks not a shadow of the softness, the irresolution, the weakness, and, yes, the absurdities which made Mama so humanly touching.

Where did this chitin come from? And this cold phlegm? I remember how as a young girl Christina would announce to me, concerning a new dress, a piece of costume jewelry, some hose, or some cosmetics she wanted, "Oh, you'll see, I'll get it. I'll get it all right!" And then she would proceed to the tactics—cajolery, tears, sulks, rage—that would so quickly bring Mama around. And Papa too. As for any protests on my part about favoritism, Christina, though four years the younger, had only to whisper "Elsie!" (after Elsie, the Borden's cow in the ads) to crush and silence me. Of course Christina refused to go to Cleveland College and live at home as I had done, but insisted on Northwestern, even though that meant draining Papa. And there it was she met and later married Tom Frederick, a goy—to Mama's delight—from Milwaukee, where she now lives.

However he may have failed with Christina, Papa did leave his mark on Aldous—that unmistakable huge, hooked Jewish nose. Otherwise Aldous took after Mama in looks and coloring, if not in temperament. And as soon as he flew from the nest and settled in New York (which was as soon as he could get through Cleveland College), he changed Davidov to Danton and had a plastic surgeon do an expensive job on that nose. And, really, what a shame!

For his nose was Aldous's one distinctive feature. Slicing it down and straightening it reduced it to the neutral standardized product,
and somehow made him appear immature, almost adolescent. It was a case of cutting off his
nose to spite his father.

Well, everybody is aware of the Oedipus
complex except, of course, poor stupid Oedipus.
Whenever I see Aldous Danton, as I do on my
occasional trips to New York, while that new
nose makes him a stranger in false-face, I can
still smell the old rancid marrow of hatred in
him, and I feel sure that my baby brother still
grinds his teeth in his sleep. And no doubt
Papa's favorite foods still nauseate him, and he
still shies away from all but safe, elderly, moth-
erly women. Having made his desperate get-
away, Aldous wards off Papa's pursuing ghost
by the obsessive order of his morbidly neat
apartment and his morbidly neat existence,
marshaling his books in rigid ranks, adjusting
a vase or a bowl one inch nigher to the unattain-
able perfection, checking and rechecking the
security of door and window, ritualistically
fingering lapel and necktie. Compared to him,

old maid though I am, I am a free and wild spirit, uncabined, uncribbed, unconfined, sans anxiety, compulsion, or tic. Poor dear Aldous, so admirably suited to his job as proofreader at that typographically fastidious publishing house, where the hobgoblin of his mind can track down inconsistencies of orthography and font.

At least there is no question whatsoever about me. I am Meyer Davidov's daughter. Or, as Papa would say, employing the affectionate if not the literal diminutive, *tochterl*. And even now Papa is as likely to call me *tochterl* as Lexie, his fond eye, by the candlelight of memory, still seeing within the hundred and sixty-seven pounds avoirdupois the little girl who ran more or less innocently to meet him at the streetcar stop and searched his pockets for the chocolate bar or bag of gumdrops he generally brought home from the Market. Nowadays, in the harsh light of the present, most of my friends, their unbleared eyes seeing the leviathan with the lumpish legs and arms, call me Alec. Yes, I would have made a fine bouncing boy. Papa bequeathed me his bodily bulk, his thick black ringlets (now, as I approach fifty, iron gray), his swarthiness, and his nose. But, alas, without his sex. And without his great gusto and hunger for life. That's where Mama unfortunately intervened to bestow upon me her girlish yearnings, timidity, shyness. Like the Wife of Bath, I was born under two conflicting planets. However, needless to say, for me there were no five husbands at church door, withouten oother compaignye in youthe.

As a little girl, of course, I was troubled by none of this. I was happy to be Papa's *tochterl*, to sit at his right hand at the table, and share his sardines afloat in vinegar, his fried herring, his chicken gizzards, his cold borsch with the islands of steaming potatoes in it, his cheese blintzes and sour cream, his baked beef liver chopped up with onions and hard-boiled eggs. It was not until later, in her unhappy adolescence, that Lexie would study the mirror and then weep bitterly through the hours of the night because of what she saw there, sobs racking her breast at the unfair unfair unfair caprices of Fortune. And always present to her eye was the precocious parallel of Christina, who began having dates at twelve, and by fourteen, I am sure, had discarded her maidenhead as excess baggage. To her that hath not shall not be given. For Lexie there were no boys and no dates, no Danceland, Crystal Slipper, or Bamboo Gardens, no foxtrotting to "Charlie My Boy" and "Button Up Your Overcoat," no necking in cars or on the porch swing, no erotic Moonlight Cruises on Lake Erie, no pinching wanton on the cheek and no reechy kisses, no new dresses and no need for them. Instead, when she didn't escape into the exotic world of Papa's store, she learned to cultivate the many cultural advantages of Cleveland—the Public Library, Wade Park and the Art Museum, the Institute, the Symphony, the Playhouse, Karamu.

I suppose, considering how Papa had stamped his likeness on me, it was not surprising that Mama always favored Christina. Yet that did hurt. And what a piece of irony. For

Christina simply used poor Mama outrageously. Whereas I was the only one of us children who really understood Mama and had some inkling of what she had gone through. How my aching heart would cry out, "Oh, Mama, I understand! At last I have grown up and I understand! Oh, I understand so much, and I love you!" Particularly during those last months when she had become quite feeble and often not lucid, and tottered aimlessly about the house with her failing heart fluttering like a big moth in her throat. Nearly every weekend I would drive in from my college in northern Ohio to spend a night or two with her. What made my bowels yearn upon her was the trapped look of her face, with its sad remote smile that never rose to those eyes tarnished by all the hopelessness of day piled on day. I felt I had somehow to make it all up to her, and I would come bearing little expiatory gifts—a silver pin (Mama loved silver), a vial of perfume, some handkerchiefs, a shawl, a set of combs.

Mama would make a show of interest as she unwrapped my gift. "Alexandra, thank you. It was nice of you to think of me, but it wasn't really necessary."

"Oh, Mama, it's nothing. Just a little token."

"What does a sick old woman want with something like this?"

"It gave me pleasure to buy it for you, Mama."

"Alexandra, you should have saved your money."

"But Mama, I wanted to let you know how much I *love* you."

And I would hug her frail wasted body to my hulk, as if I were the mother and she the child, while she would smile her sad remote smile. But try as she might, Mama could never really forgive me for being Papa's *tochterl*. Maybe at bottom she had reason. And I don't mean the reason which all of us children—even Aldous—came to know, although Mama, with her unbelievable gift for self-deception, either didn't or wouldn't know that we knew. It was merely that I could not help, by lineament, gesture, attitude, mannerism, the cut of my jib, being a reminder of Meyer Davidov. As on that day Mama said to me, "Alexandra, when my time comes, I want you to have my gold wedding band."

Could I let that go? No! Like Papa, I was never able to abide Mama's prevarication and flimflam. I couldn't allow for that dire need in her to go around the bare and barren truth. I had to say tartly (I can't forgive myself for it), "You mean, Mama, that you want Christina to have the diamonds."

# *Two*

What couldn't one of our modern academic metaphysical poets, with a headful of bogus medievalism, make of the wedding band as symbol? The golden ring as the image of wedlock, the marriage bond, *vinculum matrimonii.* The circle as the allegory of unity, harmony, perfection, self-completion. The conceit of the chaplet, the flowery garland of joy and hope, the zone of contentment. The anagogical sign of the bright wheel of love, the glorious crown of the human relationship, the mystical Blessed Sacrament. Or if our academic poet (secure in his tenure contract and his TIAA and CREF pension plans) is reveling in today's fashionable swart mood, then the wedding band becomes a noose, a yoke, a shackle, a manacle, a coop, a cage, the emblem of bondage, thralldom, confinement, durance vile. Well, as Isak Dinesen writes in one of her Gothic tales, "When you know what things are really like, you can make no poems about them." To figure forth the reality of the union of Meyer and Eleanor Davidov, the wedding band ought, by some metaphorical twist, to represent one of those lead capes in which Frederick II of Sicily had his enemies wrapped before throwing them into the red-hot caldron. Or more apt, that medieval torture which bound a ravenous wildcat inside a man's tunic to claw, tear, and bite at his entrails. Except that Papa and Mama, thus bound together for life, were each both cat and victim.

Yet all this figures forth only one side of the reality. For I do have a few memories of happy scenes too, although, I must admit, mostly in the very distant past, before Bubbeh came to live with us. And, I grant, the roseate glow may have issued from the child's heart rather than from the object contemplated. I recall evenings when the Davidovs would have their friends over, to drink hot tea out of tall glasses in the Russian manner, to reminisce about the Old Country, and to sing the many sentimental or humorous Jewish songs which they had brought to America with them or had composed out of their experiences here, songs like *"Tsu mir iz gekummen mein couzineh"* and *"Zoll zein schah, der rebbeh geht schoen schloffen."* And picnics at Euclid Beach, with the picnic basket a cornucopia of the fried chicken and potato salad and strudel Mama had cheerfully prepared, and rides on the merry-go-round and roller coaster. And twilight hours when Papa and Mama would sit together out on the porch swing, Mama gratified to have Papa's arm around her waist, and both of them gazing quietly and contentedly at the passers-by on tree-lined Phillips Avenue or conversing in low, tender voices.

*Think,* as I importune my students when I attempt to pry them out of their provincial shells and set them down in the strange and remote fourteenth century. *Think! Think!* Think of Mama going, like a bewildered immigrant, to the foreign land of Meyer Davidov's customs and associations. Think of her learning to speak and understand so alien a tongue as Yiddish. Think of her coming to cook all those unfamiliar dishes that Papa liked. Are not these the tokens of some earlier lost behavior? Evidence of a time when she must have been trying to please Papa? Or think of Mama—even before Bubbeh was there to instruct her—mastering the complicated observances of the numerous Jewish holy days. Of course, the rites were maimed. For Mama was, after all, not a Jew. And Papa cared not one bit for the religion as such, but merely took a childlike delight in the special foods, the ceremonial chants, the color and lights and festivity. Nevertheless, for every Friday evening Mama baked the plump braided *challehs* and lit the candles. And as each holy day in its turn came along, she got ready the *tayglach,* the *homentashen,* the *eingemachtz,* or the other traditional dish thereto appertaining.

How little we know our parents. Always we see them as Papa and Mama, sprung full-grown and fully clothed in the habits and characteristics we are accustomed to. From the beginning they are simply there, like the street lamps and the telephone poles, the houses and the trees. We see them as the providers of our wants, the nurses of our ills and hurts, the omniscient and omnipotent guardians of our precious little egos. We never see them as mewling, puking infants, as schoolboy and schoolgirl, as rebellious or moody adolescents, as young lovers discovering passion or quarreling jealously, as male and female in rut and oestrus. I know more about Jean Froissart or Guillaume de Machaut than I do about Meyer Davidov or Eleanor Harper. Concerning Papa and Mama in the long ago, so much is legend and hearsay, guesswork and dream work, the flimsy stuff that the scholar would disdain except for use as a curiosity in a footnote.

To employ an expression our social scientists are partial to, I have to extrapolate—and, like a crab, backwards. Since Papa came over steerage from a village in Poland carrying his earthly possessions in a small bundle tied with rope, and since Mama came without so much as a second cousin from an orphan home not far from Cleveland, we were not the species of family so common in New England, Virginia, or Philadelphia, with a rich accumulation of heirlooms ringing the changes on the family's history. Our few souvenirs gave off hardly a tinkle —the cheap brass-plated bowl with the silhouette of Niagara Falls stamped into it, or the hollow glass sphere from Cedar Point with the tiny white flakes inside falling, when it was inverted, like a minikin snowstorm. And one photograph (appropriated by me), yellowed and cracked, taken either just before or just after their marriage (there was no wedding photo). Mama is a pretty damsel of twenty-two, in the long skirt, severe shirtwaist, and high buttoned shoes of those days. Her figure is sculptured by a corset, she has a good bosom, and her hair is piled up in a coil on her head. Papa is only eighteen, stiffly posed in a new suit with a single-breasted three-button jacket, much slimmer, of course, than now, but already a robust muscular fellow, throwing off even in the faded photo an air of eagerness and vitality, the thick black ringlets cascading over his forehead, and the huge scimitar of cartilage and flesh dominating, almost overshadowing, the youthful face. From that nose, what the medieval physiognomist would have presumed about the sexual organ! I can see our Dean shaking his head in disapproval: what kind of thought is that for a proper maiden lady to entertain!

Which brings me to how Papa came to marry Mama. From questions asked, reminiscences, comments by old friends of the Davidovs, unconscious slips, I have pieced together a sort of story, the way a ruined mosaic is partially restored, with the many gaps in the picture where the original bits of colored marble or glass are missing. Papa came over at seventeen, his older brother Avrom, who had already been here a year, having sent him the passage money. Papa was part of that swarming invasion in the early years of the century, not by ruthless Vikings sailing in beaked boats and bearing shields and battle-axes but by peaceful wops, hunkies, Polacks, and kikes sailing stinking steerage and bearing shovel and pick, needle and shears. He joined Avrom in Cleveland, and they roomed together somewhere in the Thirties off Woodland Avenue. Soon he began to attend night classes for immigrants at Central High, where he learned to speak, read, and even laboriously write enough English to get along on. Mama happened to be the teacher of his class. She had finished high school and two years of normal school and this was her first job.

Perhaps it was boy meets girl. I can only weave suppositions about how Papa was taken with Mama's pretty face and figure, and no doubt awed, until he came to know better, by her display of learning and her exalted position as teacher. As for Mama, she must have been simply bowled over by Papa's sheer masculine bulk, his deep rumbling voice, his handsome build and virility. There must have been meetings, walks together, kisses (stolen or otherwise), and (given Papa) something more. At any rate, their marriage came about. It was during that benighted era when marriages were still made in Heaven and not in the marriage counselor's office. An orphan without kindred, Mama had no one to advise her about differences in age, background, religion, temperament, interests; no one to say her nay. And Papa?—Bubbeh was still back in that Polish village, Avrom was engrossed in the adventure of opening a second-hand-clothing store, and there was no customary schatchen present to arrange and guide.

That accounts, more or less, for the wedding band inscribed

But what would our modern metaphysical poet make of that tuft of scratches where the date had been scraped away? There I have the advantage. Having had as a child big ears and big eyes, I can put this two and that two together to get five. One February evening Papa came home carrying a bouquet wrapped in green tissue paper. He hugged Mama, bussed her loudly, and with a flourish handed her the flowers: "Guess what important day in our life this is, Nellie! And I brought you a little something to celebrate. From the old man to you! A happy anniversary!"

Mama was clearly pleased. And while she was eagerly tearing open the tissue paper, she said, "How nice of you to remember, Meyer. And my favorite roses! Red red roses!"

"Sure I remember! One dozen years, one dozen roses!"

Instantly the felicitous atmosphere chilled as though Papa had committed some dreadful breach of etiquette. Mama tightened her lips and gave him a sternly reproving look: "Why,

what a thing to say. How could you *say* a thing
like that? You know it's *thirteen* years, Meyer."

For a moment Papa appeared puzzled. But
then comprehension broke through on his face
and he began to laugh, until he noticed that I
was standing there with eyes wide and brain obviously busy. And he said, "I made a mistake,
Nellie! A man can make a mistake. Thirteen
years! Right! So we'll put darling sweetheart
Lexie in the bouquet and that will make thirteen beautiful roses." And he swung me up in
his arms and covered my face with kisses.

However, the cat was out of the bag, the
fat was in the fire. It didn't take an electronic
computer to calculate that months and years
didn't jibe. Papa and Mama had married in
February, whereas I was going to be twelve years
old the coming August. Simple even for Simple
Simon. Already, though so young, I was wise
enough not to press the matter. And it was in-
teresting to observe that never again would
Mama permit an occasion to be made of her
wedding anniversary. Somehow she maneuvered
to let each one pass by without notice.

Nevertheless, despite Mama's dodges,

Christina got at the truth. Trust her to smell it out. The result was that one ordinary common-place garden-variety afternoon Baby Brother was given the jolt of his life. He was then fourteen, Christina eighteen, and I twenty-two. The three of us were sitting at the dining-room table, waiting for Mama to come home from an afternoon of poker with "the girls" (yes, by then Mama had taken heavily to cards). Aldous was talking about one of his schoolmates in some classroom incident, and said, "The dumb bastard didn't even know the answer."

Unluckily, I was in one of my prim moods. "Don't say 'bastard,' Aldous."

"Why not? What's the matter with 'bastard'?"

"Well, it really means a boy whose father and mother were never married."

That was when it occurred to Christina to contribute her tidbit to the discussion. "It can be a girl too. Alec here came close to being a bastard herself."

"What do you mean?" demanded Aldous.

"Figure it out for yourself, dope. Mama

and Papa got married in February. Alec was born in August. Count it up on your six fingers. Mama damn well *had* to get married."

Aldous turned white, and said hoarsely, "You're a lousy stinking crummy liar!"

"But Aldous," I tried to reassure him, "that's nothing to get upset about. It happens all the time. They *did* get married. And anyhow I'm here just the same, with two eyes, two ears, a nose, and a mouth."

Aldous sat there for a long moment in rigid silence while the shock settled deep into him. Then he spoke in a voice strangled with hatred: "Papa is an animal! Just a big dirty animal! He must have forced poor Mama! Or raped her or something!"

Christina laughed scornfully: "Raped! Zooneleh, poor Mama was probably *dying* to be laid. Papa must have been quite a sex pot. He still is, you know."

At that, Aldous flung himself at Christina with hysterical fury, chasing her around the table and pounding at her with his fists. But after a minute or two he stopped suddenly,

while his face worked desperately to control itself. Then, breaking down into sobs, he ran out
of the house. It was shortly after this incident
that I had occasion to notice he was grinding his
teeth in his sleep.

# *Three*

It's as well Aldous didn't come back for Mama's funeral. That would have been a miserable mistake. Just as it was a mistake for him to come back for that last visit a year before Mama died. Which had been my doing, for, silly sentimental female that I am, I had persuaded Baby Brother that Mama might like to see him once more before the end. Aside from his being an escaped inmate who had made his peace elsewhere and should never have been dragged back to his oubliette, Aldous had been away too long. Sixteen years had gone by since his desperate flight. During all those years, I had been driving in frequently to visit Papa and Mama, and had become inured to the poison by gradually increased doses, so that I was not aware, until I saw it all through Aldous's horrified eyes, what a terrible decline there had been from any for-

mer prosperity. In actuality, the *real* decline
had taken place much earlier, while Aldous was
hardly more than a toddler, after the Davidovs
had inexplicably (*so inexplicably* to the puzzled little Lexie) sold their pleasant one-family
house on Phillips east of 123rd Street, and had
moved into the cramped rented downstairs
quarters of a two-family house on Fairport in
the less affluent neighborhood west of 123rd.

For one thing, the sea of Negroes, year
upon year washing steadily eastward, had finally
broken through the dike at 105th, and had in-
undated all the streets east to 123rd, leaving a
few scattered islands of forsaken Jewish families
like the Davidovs. For another, the neighborhood itself had grown dingier and dirtier. The
streets were much too crowded and noisy. Tin
cans, broken bottles, dirty scraps of paper, and
oddments of garbage ornamented the sidewalks,
gutters, and lawns. Evidently the landlords, ex-
hibiting the fine flowering of the profit motive,
were squeezing all they could out of their prop-
erties and doing nothing by way of upkeep. The
houses huddled in row after row of crippled
slovens, paint long since peeled off the clap-

boarding, roofs swayed and shingles curled or fallen, porches sagged, steps tilted and broken, trees dead or dying.

Even in those better days which Aldous had known, the neighborhood had been essentially a shabby one. The houses, all identical (both in substance *and* accident, the medievalist in me prompts me to say), were up-and-down two-family frame structures, each rooted in the barest minimum of land, with a paved driveway along one side, and a pinch of lawn in front enclosed by a blistered and rusted iron railing and occupied by a tree and some dusty clumps of plantain. Nothing picturesque, nothing quaint, no turrets, no dovecotes, no delightful irregularities and unexpected nooks, no belvedere, no distant prospects, no wash of color, no patina of history relieved the dreariness. Each house had two front porches, up and down. Each porch led directly into a small living room, behind that a smaller dining room, and behind *that* an even smaller kitchen, with a hall to one side opening on two scanty bedrooms and a bathroom. The sole concessions to the aesthetic sense were the toylike gas-burning fireplace in the living room and the leaded-glass doors on the dish cabinet, to go with the rococo cut-glass chandelier in the dining room.

But it may be that a less greedy breed of landlord existed in those earlier days. At least the houses had been given a coat of paint occasionally, and rotten clapboards and shingles had been replaced. Moreover, our house still had in it the furniture brought along from our former prosperity on Phillips. Now, however, the rugs were rubbed down in patches to the burlap backing, the davenport (which had served Aldous as bed each night) and the matching armchair were frayed and stained, the old upright piano was a crazy caricature of itself, the window curtains were torn and uneven, the dishes and silverware were remnant odds and ends, the wood on furniture and floor and molding was scratched and had flakes of ancient varnish adhering to it. Yes, our house was the true outward emblem of the life within. It was the house of the broken spirit, of persons who no longer cared. It was never a question of poverty, for Papa had always made money enough to put on a much better show. And while a Negro woman came in each Thursday to clean, and I pitched in whenever I showed up for a visit, the grime was hopelessly infused into the corners, and roaches were abroad in the kitchen. What dismay poor Aldous betrayed, coming from his sterilized existence! Appalled, he took a room at the Statler. And I recall how careful he was not to rest hands or elbows on any surface of the Davidov house.

And, of course, Papa and Mama had declined too, in crossing over to their sixties. Age and illness had crumpled Mama from a plump middle-aged woman to a feeble old lady with thin gray hair and a loose-hanging speckled skin. Age had even dared lay its uncivil hand on Papa, grizzling the hair at his temples, shrinking him an inch or two in height, and converting the mass and muscle of his body to soggy flesh and fat. What was more, his liveliness was often a matter of effort and habit rather than overflowing exuberance, and at times he dozed off after dinner like an old man. And, I must add, some of the sense of change came from the distance Aldous himself had journeyed in those intervening years. When I had urged him to make his visit, I hadn't really considered what a stranger he would appear in his Brooks Brothers suit and haberdashery, his French cuffs with the gold-and-onyx links, his white silk handkerchief sticking out the proper margin at the breast pocket, his reserved manner, and his new nose.

Papa *was* taken aback, but only for a moment. Pushing right through the sixteen years' absence, he greeted Aldous with a wet resounding kiss and enveloped his *zooneleh* warmly in his arms. There Aldous stood limp, an unwilling bride painfully enduring a passionate embrace on her first night. With the Davidov nose sliced away, he no longer looked like Papa's son but, rather, like a slender, blond, prissy gentile by some odd accident of mistaken identity finding himself hugged by a stranger in the incredible shape of a big black hook-nosed Jew. Moreover, Aldous's tidy clothes and demeanor made Papa appear, by contrast, all the more careless. Just as Papa was not a neat eater, so he was never a neat dresser. But now his shiny blue serge suit showed food stains, his trousers bagged, his white shirt was soiled at the collar and cuffs, his floral red-and-blue tie was wrinkled and much too loud. What struck me most, however, seeing Papa there with Aldous to give scale, was the seedy air about him, and an overdone heartiness, a distemper contracted during the years as salesman in one of the big cheap clothing stores downtown. Papa's own store had long since been sold, and the money gambled or frittered away. More than anything else, that sudden realization of the decline in Papa pinched my heart.

Nevertheless, there was still plenty of the old Papa left. More than enough to stir up the ancient trouble buried in Aldous, so that on his visit he avoided Papa as much as he could. Mostly he sat quietly next to Mama, awkwardly holding her hand and making an effort to carry on a conversation with her. But estrangement had set in. Besides, Mama had withdrawn into herself and had become indifferent to the people around her, as if she had said her goodbyes aboard a ship entering port and thereafter was not willing even briefly to renew the ties that must soon be broken. Well, no matter how Aldous maneuvered, Papa was not to be entirely denied. He was always one to override reticences and objections. Thus on a memorable evening, after I was done with the dinner dishes, Papa willy-nilly carried Aldous, and me too, off to Manny's, half a dozen blocks from our house.

I had been to Manny's often with Papa and knew it for a harmless neighborhood tavern, but to Aldous, poor timid Aldous, it may well have appeared a sinister den of iniquity. Manny's consisted of a long walnut bar, fluorescent lights, stools of chromium and red leatherette, a few tables, a pinball machine with dazzling electrical effects, and an illegal back room where card playing went on. Most of the drinking was beer, most of the couples were decently if not happily married, most of the single men and women were (as *I* could well understand) just trying to slough off the unbearable loneliness for an hour or two. Manny himself presided over the bar, and yet managed also to keep an eye on his take in the back room. In addition, on the counter behind the bar amid the bottles of liquor were displayed cheap costume jewelry, wrist watches, nylon stockings, black lace nightgowns, stuffed velours animals, and other such gifts as might appeal to a patron far gone in alcoholic sentiment. Manny knew how to turn every penny.

Like Papa, Manny was a big heavy-set Jew, not black-haired and swarthy however, but red-headed, fair, and immensely freckled. And like Papa, he was extravagant of gesture and voice. Both of them enjoyed growling and bellowing at each other like two playful bears. Besides, Manny was well aware that Papa was always good for a few dollars and often for an evening in the back room. As for Papa, *his* pleasure came from making his presence boisterously known. And I'm sure the other customers were happy enough for any diversion that might crack the pervading boredom. Papa and Manny were satisfied to repeat the same tried jocular exchanges and amiable insults, for it was sound and fury they were after, not content.

Thus on that evening, Papa proudly introduced me, as he invariably did, for all the tavern to hear. "Manny, I want you to meet my *tochterl,* who in Columbus's America is a college professor."

"Yes, I already had the pleasure, Miss Davidov."

"And this is my *zooneleh,* who is paying me a visit. He comes here from New York."

"Pleased to meet you," said Manny, putting out a wet paw across the bar.

Papa went right on into the vaudeville routine which I had so often heard. "Now Manny is not from New York. He comes all the way from Minsk."

"No, you're making a mistake, Davidov. Not from Minsk."

"Not from Minsk? I was sure it was Minsk."

"No, not from Minsk. And also not from Dvinsk."

"Then," roared Papa triumphantly, "it must be *Pinsk!* Zooneleh, meet Mr. Manny, who comes not from Minsk and not from Dvinsk but from Pinsk!"

"What an old man you got!" Manny confided to Aldous and me. "The joker right out of the deck!"

You can readily guess how Aldous cringed at this whole performance. And when Papa turned to him and asked, "What'll you have to drink, Zooneleh?" he replied in a finicking voice, "I believe I'll have a Scotch-and-soda."

"My *zooneleh* believes he'll have a Scotch-and-soda." Papa couldn't resist mimicking Aldous. "And a beer for my *tochterl,* and for me too." Then while Manny busied himself getting the drinks ready and setting them before us, Papa announced, "Tonight I'm celebrating because two of my darling children are with me. Manny, I'd like to buy a little something for my *tochterl.* Let's see what you got. I'm going to give you another chance to cheat me."

"Listen to the man talk," said Manny as he promptly brought out a tray of costume jewelry. "It costs me money every time he comes in here."

The tray held a galaxy of horrors. But having been through this many a time, I had learned to let Papa have his way. He was going to have it anyhow. And whatever money he squandered could, after all, be charged to his evening's entertainment. At his insistence, I picked out a necklace, the least atrocious item in the tray and the least likely to put excessive strain on the disapproving eyebrows of my spinster colleagues.

"Okay, Tochterl," said Papa, "I like that one too. You got good taste. That's from me to my darling Lexie. How much is it, Manny?"

"There's a tag on it. You can read, can't you?"

"Sure I can read. Nine-fifty! That's *nur fur die goyim*. I'll give you five dollars and you'll still be robbing me."

Manny sighed elaborately. "What a *ganof* you got for an old man, Miss Davidov. But seeing it's for you, I'm not even going to bargain with him. To show you my heart's in the right place, I'll lose money on it."

Papa laughed. "I should always lose money the same way! And now, what about a little present for my *zooneleh*?"

"Oh, no, Dad!" Aldous bleated in consternation. "I really don't need anything!"

But Manny had already produced a small royal-purple plush-lined box containing a set of cuff links and tie clasp in one of the new brassy alloys, of a monstrous design involving armorial bearings that would certainly have amazed Heralds' College. Even now I have to laugh remembering the look on Aldous's face. But his protests only prolonged the anguish. Both Papa and Manny simply called upon the other customers to approve the set as just the thing, and one old unshaven drunk came over, threw his arm around poor Aldous's shoulders, and puffed persuasion upon him with a moldy whiskey breath. Of course, after gratifying himself with the customary bout of haggling, Papa made the purchase and forced it upon Zooneleh.

Considering the acute embarrassment Aldous suffered at Manny's, I can well imagine what his pain would have been at Mama's funeral. For there Papa hogged the spotlight. Even Mama and the rabbi were upstaged. You know, *really,* Papa does belong in the Middle Ages, when the public display of violent feelings and the exaggerated expression of grief were the expected thing. I can readily picture him as one of those men who, in the medieval chronicles, held forth flamboyantly and lachrymosely for two or three hours on the scaffold before their own execution, causing the crowds of spectators to drench the ground with tears. And the orthodox Jewish ritual gave Papa's melodramatic talents full scope. He out-Heroded the hired professional mourners. And at the graveside, when Papa tore the lapel of his jacket (symbolic of the rending of one's clothes and the heaping of ashes on one's head), he did look like a dark, massive wind-blown Old Testament patriarch.

Yet what Aldous would have taken for embarrassing histrionics was something beyond that, something out of that lost and unknown world of black gabardine and cabalistic muttering Bubbeh came from. It was just a totally different mode of feeling and expression. I don't know what Christina felt as she watched that overwrought performance, but I confess that *I* was touched by Papa, and I broke down and wept when I heard him sob at Mama's grave, *"Veh iz mir! Oi, veh iz mir!* Nellie, my wife! What am I going to do without you! What am I going to do without you! Nellie! Nellie! Nellie! *Voss hubben vir gemacht fon dem lebben!* (What have we done with our life!)" Then he turned his big swarthy face streaming with tears to the friends and mourners gathered about.

*"Ai, hutt af mir rachmonis! Azay vie a chulem! Der lebben geht ferbei azay vie a chulem!"* Yes, show some pity for me! It's all just a dream! Life goes by like a dream! Prospero, as I most learnedly remind myself, says substantially the same thing.

# Four

As a matter of fact, even if Papa had not been there to put on that extravaganza, poor Aldous would have squirmed at Mama's funeral. The orthodox Jewish rites, with their unbridled groans, moans, and sobs, are not for Aldous. It's all much too primitive. Now *his* decorum would be completely at home in the restrained and dignified obsequies we academics go in for—something, say, with a few commemoratory speeches in Wardour Street prose awkwardly mumbled by friends of the deceased to the subdued accompaniment of a reedy funeral-parlor organ. I may be an old-maid schoolteacher full of cranks and crotchets, yet I feel there is much to be said for all the orthodox Jewish weeping and wailing, including even those decibels of lamentation contributed by the hired professional mourners. Of *course* it's barbaric. However, death is barbaric too. And the one who dies ought not to be put away quietly, without so much as a passing bell, almost hugger-mugger, as if no more were involved than an afternoon tea or an informal reception. Oh, that way, I realize, everybody concerned suffers the least discomfiture. But damn it all, someone dies, there ought to be an uncivilized yawp! You ought to make a great big noise! Maybe shoot off twenty-four cannons! Or at the very least some giant firecrackers! Well, I suppose it *would* give us an awful headache to have all those cannons and firecrackers banging away every hour of the day and night.

I'm sure other aspects of Mama's funeral would likewise have made Aldous uncomfortable. Take the burial ground itself. Papa and Mama belonged to one of those Jewish societies in which immigrants from the same region of the Old Country banded together, partly for mutual protection, insurance, and benefit, partly for fellowship and entertainment. Among other things, the society had bought a small plot of land for a cemetery, in the remote southwest environs of Cleveland. An iron picket fence closed off the plot from the surrounding fields, but there was little as yet to call to mind the smooth green turf rolling gently over the mounds in a venerable established cemetery. Indeed, this was an unkempt graveyard, showing more weeds than grass. But such as it was, these wandering Jews from Poland and Lithuania, stranded on foreign soil and often alienated from their children, who no longer spoke Yiddish and many of whom were married to the accursed goyim, made it their final resting place. At least there these lost souls had a piece of earth in which they could huddle together, and back and side wouldn't have to go bare. Already a considerable scattering of raw ragged mounds marked those who had fallen by the wayside. Each member of the Society had an assigned space. Right next to Mama's was Papa's. And on the other side of Papa's, by special dispensation, was mine. Of course, Christina and Aldous wouldn't be caught dead there.

Yes, and another thing. Take Mama lying there in the coffin. Would Aldous have been able to recognize her? Even to *me* she seemed a stranger. It was mostly, I suppose, the way the undertaker had fixed her up, and particularly the rouge on her cheeks. For aside from some modest powder, Mama had always worn a plain unvarnished face. Well, "always" is not strictly accurate. I do remember, back in our house on Phillips, standing and watching with a little girl's fascination as Mama put on lipstick and rouge, and touched perfume to her ears, throat, hair, eyebrows, and arms. (It was when we moved to Fairport and the family fortunes began to crumble that she gave up all such "silly nonsense," as she came to call it.) Laid out in the pink quilted-satin lining of the coffin, and wearing that unaccustomed rouge, Mama appeared positively *lewd,* a depraved old woman cutting a last wicked caper. It was as though the undertaker had somehow penetrated to the fantastic delusion of her last days and, in the manner of an Expressionist painter, had objectified what was going on in her poor crazed brain. At the same time, while Mama's face appeared lewd, it remained unhappy. Even though her sad eyes were shut, and notwithstanding all the undertaker's sprightly art, the lines of her face and the sagging corners of her mouth gave

Mama the hopeless look I was so familiar with.

As Christina and I stood beside the coffin looking down into it (I spare my chafed vanity the details of the grotesque contrast we sisters presented), I said, "Poor Mama! She always was so unhappy. The cheerfulness was all squeezed out. There was never any sparkle or fun in her. Only this sad, remote, heartbreaking look."

Christina replied acidly, "Poor Mama was a sap!"

"*De mortuis nil nisi bonum.*"

"Okay, *Professor* Davidov. We all know you got your Ph.D."

"Remember the occasion, Christina, and try for once not to be pissy. Why do you think Mama was a sap?"

"Only a sap would take the kind of beating she took from Papa day after day and year after year."

"It wasn't *all* Papa's fault," I protested. "I'm sure something could be said on his side. And anyhow, you know Papa. A creature of appetites and impulses. What could poor Mama do? He's not so easy to manage."

"I bet *I'd* have brought him to heel damn fast!"

I looked at Christina, thinking, with a pang of envy, how striking her slim blondness appeared in black, and what a seductive thing she had made even of mourning, with the little black veil over her eyes, the white gloves, the alluring panels of fagoting set into the bodice of her dress, and the downright sexy black suède shoes. "Yes," I agreed, "you probably would. And I guess your way makes everything just dandy for the wife. But what does it do to the husband?"

"I can tell you one thing it does!" she declared impatiently, her scornful eyes sweeping me from ghastly hastily purchased black hat to shapeless low-heeled shoes, and underlining each unattractive feature of my ungainly bulk. "I would have done something with Papa. The kind of man he is, he should have made a stir in the world. And a pile of money too! He had personality, magnetism, vigor. He had the stuff for a big success. Then why didn't he ever move on up? I'll tell you why. Because of Mama. Like most men, Papa is lazy, and ready to settle for a good meal and a piece of tail. Mama never gave him the push he needed. She let it all dribble away. Just look at him now! Tom hasn't got half of Papa's stuff. But you can bet your hat—wherever in the world did you get it?—that *my* husband isn't going to end up selling men's suits and topcoats in that cheap store."

However, to get away from Christina's improper coffin-side remarks and back to Aldous. What a shock it would have been for him to see Mama during those last months. His visit fortunately came *before* she went to pieces. Even then, he made no contact. How could he? All his feelers, peepers, and twitchers were turned inward. He performed the filial duty expected of him. He held her hand and he spoke some words. But love? Compassion? Some outflowing of feeling? No. No. No. I do put it cruelly, but this sick old woman out of whose womb he once came forth to greet the Sun was merely a nuisance, a vexation which had torn him out of his life-preserving routine and set him back amid the ancient terrors of Cleveland. And *after* Mama failed so suddenly—but I don't mean to be hard on Aldous. He is sick enough too, in his fashion. But the feeble wasted Mama tottering from chair to chair, given to spells of amnesia, and babbling in the reaches of the past would only have annoyed him. And her loss of control over the bodily functions (poor Mama's clothes had to be changed three and four times a day) would have disgusted him. By the best of luck, I happened on Mrs. Gastineau, a Negro woman living only three houses down on Fairport. She came in to look after Mama during the week, and I drove in to take over for the weekends.

And, finally, what would Aldous have made of the delusions? Of course, I never wrote to him about *those*. Nor did I mention them to Christina. Or to Papa either, for that matter. They certainly buckled and wrenched my sense of reality as I tossed back and forth each weekend between my sedate, hushed college community and the clamorous warrens of Fairport Avenue. *My* introduction to one of the delusions came at second hand from Mrs. Gastineau. One morning she had taken Mama out to sit in the porch swing, and had gone back into the house to straighten things up, only to discover that Mama had wandered off somewhere. Fortunately, most of the Negroes in the neighborhood knew who she was, and one of them led her back home. Mrs. Gastineau could make very little of her incoherence, except to gather that Mama was searching, however ineffectually, for some definite place and often stopped someone on the street or rang a doorbell to ask her way. These wanderings of Mama's became alarmingly frequent.

On a Friday early in May, I drove in as usual after my one-thirty class in Chaucer, and as I came up Lakeview to turn into Fairport, I saw Mama in a house dress, stumbling along on the sidewalk. I pulled up to the curb, got out of the car, and ran after her. "Mama!" I cried as I caught her arm. She turned a startled look on me. "Mama! Don't you know me?"

"Of course I know you, Alexandra. How silly you are!"

"Well, what are you doing out here?"

"I'm looking for my lovely house."

"But Mama, it's right around the corner

there on Fairport."

"I *know* where my house is!" Mama said peevishly. "It's on Sillups."

"Sillups?"

"Oh, Alexandra, what's the matter with you today? And you a college professor! Not Sillups! Fipps!"

Of course, then I got it. "You mean the house on *Phillips,* Mama."

"That's what I *said*. Phillips! I simply must get there, Alexandra, before that filthy old woman ruins everything."

I knew instantly whom she meant. "Bubbeh?" I exclaimed. "Why, Bubbeh—"

"I'm late already, Alexandra. The lilacs are out and I must cut enough to fill all the vases. Oh, it's such a lovely lovely house. Seven big rooms full of air and sunlight. And you know that real brick fireplace in the living room to burn logs in, and the nice wide kitchen with the maple cabinets and the serving pantry, and the big front hall with the staircase going up to the bedrooms. And now the wonderful fragrance of the lilacs will be coming in the bedroom windows all through the night."

I put my arms around her. "I'll take you to the house on Phillips tomorrow, Mama. I promise you."

She strained with all her little strength to break loose. "No, I must get there right away, or that horrible old woman will ruin everything!"

"I'll see to it that Bubbeh doesn't touch a thing. Just leave it to me. But now we have to go back, or Mrs. Gastineau will be worried. She's a nice lady, Mama. You don't want her to be worried, do you?"

And I led Mama back to the house on Fairport. As we turned up the walk, she cried out, "Why are you bringing me *here?*"

"This is where you live, Mama."

"No, no. I don't want to come here. This ugly place is *not* my house!"

But she was so feeble she was unable to resist, and I led her up the steps to the front porch and sat with her in the swing. She began to weep weakly. "Why did you bring me here?"

"Mama, you live here." And I rocked her in my arms.

"No, I don't!" she sobbed. "This is not my

house. It's such a mean, ugly, crowded place. The furniture is old and broken. And it's so dirty everywhere. There are *roaches* in the kitchen. It's a disgrace. And why am I living on a street with these *schvartzeh* that I don't know? Where are all my friends?"

"Mama darling! Mama darling! Mama darling!" I rocked her until all the weeping and sobbing stopped.

# Five

While I comforted the frail Mama darling who sobbed like a heartbroken child for the lovely house with its garland of lilac bushes that she had lost somewhere on Sillups, and while I shielded her from the terrors of Bubbeh, little did I realize what other *fantastical* Mama I was rocking in my arms. I first encountered that *other* delusion, that murky concupiscent vapor arising from Mama's poor cracked head, only a month before Mama died. Of course, if in the medieval manner we are taking account of First Causes, Papa brought out the bitch in every woman he came near. Even Mama. Yes, even Mama crept out of the jungle hidden behind the formal garden of her proprieties and pruderies. I suppose that there are men who, like stallions or bulls, have the sexual force to set up a kind of magnetic field. As Christina would be ever so quick to point out, an old-maid schoolteacher can't be expected to know about such arcane matters.

But how many many times I have seen Papa come into a room, to have his presence instantly sensed by every woman there. It was as though a magnificent swarthy Semitic chieftain had come in wearing a burnoose, and vibrant with virility. Every woman appeared under compulsion to look up and gauge the arrogant head with its hawk nose and black ringlets, the massive chest and shoulders, the thick arms and thighs crowding the seams of sleeve and trouser. Perhaps Papa gave off a musk. Perhaps his sheer bulk caused a displacement of the air. Whatever it was, there it would be—the covert glance and the slight faltering in the conversation of even the most proper and self-contained woman. And sooner or later, nearly every woman in the room would be irresistibly drawn to Papa, to talk too much, laugh too loud, roll her eyes foolishly, and find some pretext to touch him or, if bolder, to run a hand through his hair.

It occurs to me that Lexie was not always so detached and objective an observer. Like poor Mama, she had to get used. And how the Stations of the Cross throng to mind! But perhaps two epiphanies (a term presently favored by the literary quarterlies) will suffice to suggest how Lexie came to learn acceptance. In the first, she is seven or eight, and is happily sitting across from Papa at a small table covered with a red-and-white checkered cloth which bears the ancient and honorable stains of wine and food. They are having lunch together in Joe Saluzzo's corner saloon-restaurant, not far from Uncle Avrom's and Papa's store, in that region south of downtown Prospect, where the east-west streets, such as Central, Scovill, and Woodland, and the north-south streets, such as Ontario, Broadway, and Ninth, all warp and converge into a snarl because of the sharp bends taken by the deep valley of the Cuyahoga River. It is a crowded, bustling district of rickety out-of-plumb and out-of-plumbing tenements, commission houses dealing in fruits and vegetables, wholesalers in textiles and leather goods, second-hand stores of all sorts, pawnshops, saloons, cheap restaurants, low-priced whorehouses, and a litter of outdoor stalls (Cleveland's Marché aux Puces), all dominated by the vast old covered Market where every kind of food and produce can be bought. The crisscross of streets and alleys is medieval in its crush, noise, smells, and filth.

Lexie has come down to the store in the morning by streetcar with Papa, as he permits her to do now and then on Saturdays. For her, it is all a delightful adventure, as well as an eye opener on the ways of the adult world, giving her a chance to wander through the exciting tangle of streets and along the aisles of the Market, and even down into the inferno of the Cuyahoga Valley far below. Most of all, she loves eating at Joe Saluzzo's, with the men at the bar laughing and shouting back and forth in a babel of broken English and outlandish tongues. She loves the strange, strongly flavored Italian food —the *minestrone* thick with barley and unfamiliar vegetables, the veal awash in its savory tomato sauce, the fried zucchini, the spaghetti laden with nuggets of cheese—and the sour red wine which Papa lets her sip out of his thick tumbler.

As they sit there, the waitress, a fleshy slatternly blonde with washed-out blue eyes, comes over to the table to take their order. "Hello there, Tall-Dark-and-Handsome," she says to Papa. Then she ruffles Lexie's hair. "Your little sister is a good-looker just like you."

Lexie doesn't care for that tone or manner, not one bit, and she withdraws her head. Papa laughs. "This? This is my *tochterl*, my little daughter, my darling little Lexie!"

"Go away, you're kidding me! You're not old enough to have a daughter like this." (Of course, as I now realize, Papa was only twenty-five or twenty-six, and must have seemed far too young to be the father of a biggish girl of seven or eight.) The waitress rests her arm on Papa's shoulders and coils her fingers in those glistening black ringlets, and Papa puts his arm around her buttocks. "You're not so bad-looking yourself. How's my sweetheart today?"

Lexie, in a sudden rage, gets out of her chair and pushes the waitress violently aside. "She's *not* your sweetheart, Papa. *I'm* your sweetheart!" Then, amid the laughter of the men at the bar nearby, she hugs Papa and buries her

head in his lap. "I'm your *only only* sweetheart!"


So much for the first epiphany. Now for
the second. Lexie is eleven, and although they
have been living in the house on Fairport for
several months, she is still perplexed and troubled by the abrupt unaccountable change. It
grieves her that they sold their nice big house
on Phillips, where she had her own room with
her own bed, dresser, and closet, and moved to
this little rented box, where everything is so
cramped and she has to share a bed with Christina. She wakes up with a start in the black middle of a winter night to the shivaree of the wind
against the window frames and the sharp gun-
shots of the wood in the bedroom shrinking
with the cold. A great uneasiness swells within
her. She climbs out of bed without waking
Christina, slips her feet into the fleece-lined
warmers, goes out of the bedroom in her flannel
nightgown, and shuts the door behind her. The
little hallway is dimly lighted by a naked bulb

in the ceiling. The door to Papa's and Mama's bedroom is open, and Lexie peers in anxiously. She can make out baby brother Aldous in his crib in one corner, but the bed itself is empty. In fact, Papa's pillow has clearly not been slept on. Then Lexie becomes aware of a light emanating from the living room. She hurries out there, to find Mama wearing her nightgown and wrapper and sitting alone on the davenport in the glow cast by the small fringed table lamp. It seems to her that Mama has been crying. But Mama says sharply, "Alexandra, what are you doing out of bed?"

"Mama, where's Papa?"

"You'd better get right back to bed. You'll catch cold out here in your nightgown."

"Isn't Papa *here?*"

"He hasn't come home yet," Mama says, tacking on a false little laugh to show there is nothing to worry about. Strangely, with all her practice and all her propensity, Mama to the end of her days remained a poor liar.

"But Mama, don't you even know where he *is?*"

"Oh, it's all right. He'll be home soon."

Lexie frowns at Mama's lack of concern, and then strides out to look at the clock in the kitchen. She returns to face Mama with an eleven-year-old's determination. "Mama, it's half past *three!* Maybe Papa is sick or got into an accident!"

"Don't be silly, Alexandra."

"But how can you *know?*" Lexie goes to the front window and looks out into the winter night. "It's snowing hard. Maybe Papa fell down somewhere and broke a bone or something. Or maybe he got into a holdup like Uncle Avrom and got shot. Mama, you can't just *sit* there! You ought to call the hospitals! Or the police!"

"Alexandra, you just do what I tell you and go back to bed. You're getting yourself upset over nothing."

Lexie looks at Mama with annoyance, and then starts for the dining room, where the phone is. Mama demands, "What are you doing?"

"I'm going to call the police."

As Lexie lifts the receiver, Mama jumps up, scurries over, jerks it away from her, and puts it back on its hook. Lexie confronts her in anger: "But you don't know where Papa *is!*"

"Of course I do. He's spending the night at the Turkish bath." When Lexie purses her lips in disbelief, Mama is weak enough to add, "The one he always goes to, on Fifty-fifth, not far from Woodland."

Lexie has no doubt that this is a lie. However, she now apprehends that Mama does have some idea where Papa is, but is not going to say. And after scowling at Mama for a minute or two, she goes reluctantly back to bed and finally falls asleep.

The next evening, as soon as Papa comes home, Lexie runs to greet him. "Papa, we were worried about you. Where *were* you all last night?"

Before Papa can reply, Mama is on the scene to forestall, preclude, and avert. "Meyer, did you have a good night at the *Turkish bath?*" (Emphasis, as we scholars like to say, not mine but Mama's.)

Trust Papa to catch on fast. He hesitates for only a moment, while his sardonic eyes measure Mama and Lexie standing there before him. Then he laughs. "Yes, I had a good night. As a matter of fact, I had a wonderful night! The

Turkish bath was just what the doctor ordered! It made a new man out of me." And guffawing, he gives Lexie a suffocating hug. "How is my darling darling Lexie?"

Lexie catches on fast too. Thereafter Papa's visit to the "Turkish bath" is repeated at frequent intervals, but she never presses her anxious questions again. She now understands many things, including what that old couch is doing in the basement of Papa's store. What is odd, however, is that not once does she hear a word of complaint or remonstrance or recrimination out of Mama. No, not once. It is not a matter of indifference, for, as Lexie well knows, Mama spends many a night sitting alone on the davenport quietly, but not the less bitterly, weeping. Then what was it? Was it (what would undoubtedly be Aldous's view) praiseworthy contempt for the big dirty animal? Or (Christina's view) some bizarre manifestation of the martyr complex? Or was it simply the married woman's cowardly fear of being thrown out to earn her own living in the cold cold world? For a long time Lexie was puzzled. Only much later, much much later, did she come to the real reason (or was there still another underneath that one?) for Mama's long-suffering silence.

Well, to get along to the delusion itself, to which all of this has been, as Chaucer's Friar says, a long preamble of a tale. It was, as I have already indicated, a month before the sad end. By then poor Mama was bedridden. I had come in as usual for the weekend, to sleep on a cot near her bed and look after her. Papa had long since been moved over to the room which Christina and I had once shared. That night Mama had slept fitfully, and with many a whimper, so that the next day I allowed her to doze well on toward noon. I was alone with her, Papa having gone to work and Mrs. Gastineau having taken the weekend off. When Mama woke up finally, and after I had straightened the bed and shaken out the pillows, and had helped her brush her teeth, wash her face and hands, and comb her hair, I brought her a bowl of farina on a tray. "Well, Mama, you certainly pounded your ear."

"Why, Alexandra, I didn't sleep a wink last night."

"You didn't?" I humored her. "Why not?"

"Because of that terrible man."

"But Papa didn't even come into your room all night."

"No, not here, Alexandra. At the Comme Il Faut."

Of course, then I knew instantly what I was up against. Some precinct in Mama's poor brain was dancing a crazy little jig all its own. The Comme Il Faut, I should explain, is the Chambord, the Tour d'Argent, of Cleveland Heights, with an exaltation of elegance that mustered the middle-class Jewish women there for those refined luncheons beginning with a fruit cup in chrome green, peony pink, lemon yellow, and oyster white, and concluding with mint candies in apple green, salmon pink, primrose yellow, and ivory white. (Yes, I *am* being snotty, and in what but a trifling accident of expendable cash do these middle-class Jewish women differ from the *haut monde* so desirous of being seen at "21" or Maxim's?) Papa, I am sure, never set foot in the Comme Il Faut. But Mama was exactly the kind of woman for whom it had come into being, and she resorted there often for a luncheon with the girls before an afternoon card party.

As I studied Mama, so frail and sallow, sitting up in bed with the breakfast tray on her lap, curiosity prompted me to ask, "You mean Papa took you to the Comme Il Faut?"

"Of course not, Alexandra. You know perfectly well your father never goes there. It was that nice Mr. Rossiter who invited me."

"*Mr. Rossiter!*" I couldn't help exclaiming. And the turning up of that specter after nearly forty years made me exclaim again, "Mr. *Alan Rossiter!*"

"Oh, he's a real gentleman!" Mama went on, not even conscious of my astonishment. "He has such fine manners, Alexandra! He is always so polite, and always knows just the right thing to say and the right thing to do. And so nicely dressed! Always in the best of taste! There is never anything loud about *him*. He is so refined. His hands are always so clean and his fingernails have such beautiful half-moons. *Such* a cultured voice, and always saying things to make you feel so good! Oh, he's a knight in shining armor, Alexandra! And he was wearing the most beautifully tailored evening suit with a white tie, and of course over it all an elegant Inverness cape."

"What were *you* wearing, Mama?"

"What *would* I be wearing, Alexandra? Why, the wine-colored velvet! You know it's the only evening gown I have."

I had half expected *that*. And I could see the dress vividly across the four decades that stretched back to our house on Phillips. The occasion had been a formal dinner and musicale given by Papa's and Mama's Society in a rare access of *ton*. Nine-year-old Lexie had been as excited as Mama when that glamorous gown was delivered. It left the arms and shoulders and much of the bosom bare, and it swept to the floor in a cascade of the most graceful drapes and folds. I'm sure it was the one and only evening gown poor Mama ever had in all her life.

"But Mama," I protested, "the Comme Il Faut isn't even open after ten o'clock."

"Oh yes, it is! At eleven it becomes a night club and it stays open till three o'clock in the morning. Just like the song. That's when they have the dance floor.''

''The dance floor?''

''Why, of course. And they have only the very best name bands there. Oh, it's expensive, Alexandra, with a cover charge and a floor show and cigarette girls and favors for the ladies. It's always *very* crowded.''

''Well, you must have had a nice time, Mama.''

''Yes, I did, I did. Until I was forced to get up on the table before all those people.''

''Up on the table!'' I said. ''Who forced you, Mama?''

''That terrible man, your father.''

''Oh, Mama, *really* now!''

''Yes, Alexandra. He came into the Comme Il Faut brandishing a long whip. And his eyes were red, the way they get, you know. And he drove that nice Mr. Rossiter away. Of course he knew Mr. Rossiter is too much of a gentleman to make a vulgar scene. And then that terrible man made me get up on the table.''

''What did he do *that* for, Mama?''

''I'm ashamed to have to tell you, Alexandra. He forced me to do a strip tease. Think of it! Yes, a strip tease in front of all those stran-gers. *'I have the honor to present the charming and beautiful Mlle. Eleanor Harper, the Toast of Two Continents!'* That's what he announced. Like a barker, you know. Then he cracked his whip again and again until I had taken off every last stitch. And the lights grew dimmer and dim-mer, and his eyes kept getting redder and red-der! Just like two live coals glowing in the dark!"

At that point, either the old-maid school-teacher lost her nerve, or prudishness suddenly took possession of her, for I said sharply, "Mama, you'd better eat your farina before it gets stone-cold!"

# Six

Enter the knave of hearts. Yes, think of Mr. Rossiter thus popping up from some fissure in Mama's cracked brain! And with such befitting theatricality! Out of the submerged past, Mr. Rossiter of Inverness! Or so he must have told poor innocent Mama, whose fantasy cell, out of its overflowing wardrobe of romantic habiliments and perukes, endowed him with the Inverness cape. Mr. Alan Rossiter, who used to call me his braw bonny lassie with the same preposterously stagy burr which would round off "Eleanor" with such a fine roll when he addressed Mama. In all those years his name had not been spoken until the revenant made his phantom appearance at the Comme Il Faut. But *I* had not forgotten him. And somewhere in me I must have known that Mama had not forgotten. Nor had Papa.

78

To this day I can never look at a newspaper or magazine ad for a balmacaan or for raglan sleeves without summoning up Mr. Alan Rossiter, the way a crumb of *petite madeleine* summoned up things past for Proust. No, that is not at all appropriate. It is more the way Mephistopheles steps forth out of a puff of stage smoke, especially in one of these modern productions of *Faust,* with Mephistopheles got up as a *boulevardier* in tails and top hat and a cape lined in scarlet satin—the incarnation not of real evil but of a stage evil that it would seem anyone, even an infant, could see through. Anyone, that is, except poor deluded Mama. Oh, what fools fools fools these mortals be! How often we see someone among our friends infatuated with a man or woman so patently fake, so palpably phony, so flagrantly done up in mustachio or eyeshadow that the gay seducer or brazen hussy couldn't get away with playing the part in the shoddiest road company! Obviously the evil agent does not reside in Mephistopheles. The poor victim is the victim of his own victimization.

Whom God hath here joined together, let no man put asunder. A superfluous injunction.

The wedding band held firm against the Scottish burr, the flattering tongue, the dapper figure, the sandy mustache, the light-blue eyes. But Mama didn't. And it would have done no good to shake her by the shoulders, crying, like Hamlet, "Look here upon this picture, and this." For the mildewed ear was not Mr. Rossiter. Rather it was some romantic notion planted in Mama during her orphanage days of silly reading and girlish dreaming, a notion to which the papier-mâché Mr. Rossiter made his fatal appeal. After all, Papa was, like Eliot's hippopotamus, only flesh and blood. And how could poor foolish Mama have chosen between the two pictures? The one, she failed to see for the fabricated fictive figment it was. The other, even though she fed it by day and slept with it by night, remained an alien presence, part riddle, part bugbear.

To cite an example. Mama did not really know how Papa made his living. Think of it! Oh, she knew that he had a men's-clothing store of sorts, and vaguely where it was located. Yet she did not know (nor, for that matter, did Aldous or Christina) how he actually went about his business and what the day-to-day proceeding was, by what means the shekels came into the till. Now, in my beloved dirt-ridden down-to-earth Middle Ages that could not have happened—neither on the land, where the wife and Molyn the cow would have slept under the same thatched roof, nor in the town, where Perkyn and the other apprentices and all the tools and hubbub of the craft would have been the wife's immediate ménage. But our daily bread might as well have fallen like manna from Heaven. Yes, I doubt that Mama once set foot in Papa's store. And perhaps that was just as well. For Papa's business of buying and selling second-hand clothes would have been degrading, if not abhorrent, to her.

All this struck me forcibly one warm spring afternoon several years ago, before Mama became so very sick. I used to think up ways to entertain and interest her on my weekend visits, and I had decided to show her something of the Cuyahoga Valley, which she was even more ignorant of than most Clevelanders, who see it only as a toyland, put together out of a child's Mechano Set, far below them when they drive over the Superior High-Level Bridge. I had announced over the phone, "Mama, get yourself dressed up and ready. When I come in this afternoon, we're going for a boat ride."

"That will be nice, Alexandra. On the lake?"

"No, Mama. I thought I'd take you for a journey on Cleveland's Tiber." (An old maid must be allowed her arch humor.)

There had been a pause while Mama made the connection. "Oh, you mean the Cuyahoga. That will be nice too."

That "nice" should have warned me. Familiar as I was, from my childhood rambles, with the grime and stink of the Cuyahoga and its valley, it had not occurred to me to tell Mama what to wear. And when I came in to pick her up, I found that she had garbed herself in a flowery spring organdy, something akin to a garden dress, including even a fillet (*that,* at least, I persuaded her to take off), and was ready for a boating party on the Thames to the sweet concord of Handel's "Water Music." Of course, that was thickheaded of me. I should have realized that Mama might as well have been a tourist about to take a gondola ride on the Grand Canal. Indeed, the Cuyahoga was more foreign to her. For she had undoubtedly seen pictures of the Grand Canal. Whereas there was nothing in her experience to prepare her for that ride in the little sightseeing launch on the streaked and mottled brownish-greenish-purplish-blackish ooze of industrial waste which has usurped the bed of the Cuyahoga.

I gazed around me, enthralled as in my childhood by the scabby barges and freighters, the drawbridges and cranes and overhead tracks, the mountains of ore, sand, sulphur, and slag, the tanks, refineries, furnaces, and mills standing about like giant contortionists, the chimneys and spouts and drains incessantly excreting and discharging smoke, flame, juice, and curd of the most violent colors. It was a lurid, clangorous scene battering and bruising all my senses. Yet I felt an elation. I felt that I had my hands on the naked beating heart of the city. And then suddenly I saw poor Mama cowering there beside me, collapsed and shrunk into herself, so bewildered, revolted, *wretched* that she had even given up trying to brush the flakes of soot from her hair and dress. Callous though it may have been, at that moment I couldn't help considering how lucky it was for little Lexie that Mama did not have any inkling of what Papa's store and its environs were like. For Lexie might never have found a refuge in her unhappy adolescence. She might never have been allowed to accompany Papa on Saturdays, and might never have roamed so enraptured through the maze of alleys and byways bordering the river.

As I looked up from the launch, I could see little Lexie standing for the first time on the eastern brim of the valley and gazing down with a wild surmise upon that fiery thaumaturgy. Notwithstanding all the industrial trappings, the valley had something of a rustic aspect. It may have been only that the steep sides had sprouted a wilderness of tall weeds, a no man's land between the industrial below and the commercial above. And up on the height there at little Lexie's back was all the bustle of a medieval fair. In that Cheapside of Cleveland with the sprawling old Market for its hub, most of the chaffer took place out of doors. Pedestrians had to tread a narrow and tortuous passageway walled in by the wooden crates of oranges, grapefruits, pineapples, eggs, the wooden boxes of lettuce, melons, cabbages, grapes, the baskets of apples, tomatoes, peaches, pears, the sacks of potatoes and onions, the bunches of bananas, the mounds of watermelons or pumpkins, the stalls and the stands.

Little Lexie wandered all over, like a puppy, sniffing, nuzzling, tasting. From the dark interiors of the wholesale and commission houses came the pungent smells of cheeses, coffee, garlic, herbs, and spices. Inside the Market itself, the butchers, their hands, arms, and aprons incarnadined, cut up the fresh dripping sides of beef. And everywhere were wagons and trucks unloading and loading while men cursed and quarreled, laughed and shouted. There was even plenty of impromptu street entertainment —perhaps not jongleurs and tregetours and other such medieval mountebanks, but a terrier cornering and killing one of the huge rats that infested the region, a bit of haggling turning into a fist fight, a whore picking up some trade, and, particularly on Saturday afternoons, the men lurching along in all the stages of lamb-drunk, lion-drunk, ape-drunk, and sow-drunk.

As in medieval London, each nation had its trade or craft. Thus jobbing in fruits and vegetables fell to the Italians, and the dingy secondhand stores and pawnshops to the Jews. Actually, Papa had begun as a peddler for Uncle Avrom, buying up old clothes in the villages and towns of Ohio, Indiana, and western New York and Pennsylvania. Then (I was eight at the time) a holdup man shot and killed Uncle Avrom. Papa took over the store, but he never changed the frayed lettering across the fly-specked show window:

AVROM AND MEYER DAVIDOV

MENS WEAR

Flanking the walls inside stood the racks made of iron tubing on which hung the secondhand suits, overcoats, topcoats, and jackets that constituted the staple. Down the center ran two long tables, one with secondhand shoes ranged on it in pairs, the other supporting piles of secondhand trousers as well as new moleskins, corduroys, denims, and other such work pants. A showcase in front, together with some shelves on the wall nearby, contained the haberdashery. At the back of the store, screened by a rack of suits and coats, was the work space, holding the sewing machine, the big, broad, sturdy tailoring table, the pressing stand, and the twenty-pound goose with the long flexible tube to convey the gas to its abdominal jets.

Most of the stores, like Papa's, shared itinerant tailors and pressers who would come in for two or three days each week to put into marketable shape the old clothes bought from the peddlers. I can see plump, merry little Louie the tailor, perched cross-legged in the center of the big table like a chubby Buddha amid his shreds and patches, threading a needle, mending or altering the garment spread across his lap, biting off the ends of the thread. And I can see the face of our Negro presser wavering, like a black jinni's, in the steam arising from the sizzling press cloth. His name was Jackson Fowler, and to him clung the smell of cleaning fluid and hot damp wool. To my childish amazement, he had learned to speak Yiddish, and he would address me with mock seriousness, and without regard for grammatical gender, as *Genosse* Alexandra, allowing me to squeeze the biceps of his right arm, which had grown to prodigious size from constantly lifting and wielding the heavy goose.

This was the world (to Mama, a Dark Continent) in which Papa spent nearly all his waking hours. It was a world of haggling and trickery and knavery, where *caveat emptor* was the law of survival—in short, it was the age-old world of commerce, whose sharp practice has in our day been so slickly coated over with the hard gloss of Madison Avenue. The chaffering would begin with the peddlers, who would lug in their blue canvas sacks stuffed with the old clothes for which they had traded off cheap pots and pans or, as a last resort, paid out petty cash. Papa would scrutinize each garment in the lot with a quick expert eye while the peddler stood at his side and chanted in Yiddish, "Just take a look at the piece of goods there. You don't see a worsted like that every day. And as good as new. The fellow didn't wear that suit over a month."

To which Papa would reply, "What idiot is going to buy a double-breasted these days? And did you maybe have a look at the seat of the pants? That fellow must have spent the whole month sliding on his behind."

"That? A little patch, and you won't be able to see it."

"Some patch! Out of that patch you could make a whole suit of clothes with two pair of pants!"

And then, starting at two extremities of price so far apart as to seem impossible of compromise, Papa and the peddler would higgle-haggle dime by dime and nickel by nickel to a meeting place. In the same way, the customers who came to that region to do their shopping had learned to poke down under the top layers of fruit or vegetables, to carry each secondhand item out into the daylight for a careful examination, to look behind every label and tag which might conceal a tear or a defect. And only a *goyisher narr,* a gentile fool, would have paid the asking price without prolonged bargaining. Well, the deals were not big and the stakes were not high, but there was no doubt that Papa relished the duping and bluffing and outguessing as though it were a stock-market operation or a game of poker.

In this world of Papa's, Lexie acquired her citizenship and came to be almost as well known as Meyer Davidov himself. For from the age of seven or eight through her days at Glenville High School and even well into her course at Cleveland College, she would go down by street-car nearly every Saturday, and occasionally on other days also, to help Papa. In time the show-case and shelves of haberdashery became hers to preside over. In addition, she would sweep out the store with the long-handled push broom, keep an eye on the outdoor stand, and run to Joe Saluzzo's to bring back a schooner of beer for Papa. Yes, I am well aware of Aristotle's dictum concerning a beginning, a middle, and an *end!* My gentle reader will, I am sure, forgive me for dwelling so fondly on those happy happy days into which Lexie escaped from the harrowing presence of Christina and all the giggling girls at Glenville High and at Cleveland College who were so wrapped up in boys and dates and the sweet vanities of dress.

\* \* \*

And now for the vignette to which all this more or less necessary exposition has been a prelude. Aldous is thirteen and, having just been *bar mitzvah,* has entered upon a pimply and quavery manhood. We are having dinner, and Papa, half proudly, half mockingly, toasts Aldous in sour red wine, a bottle of which Joe Saluzzo has presented him for the occasion: "So my *zooneleh* is now a man! *Mazeltov!* I never thought I'd see the day! Well, this calls for something special. What can I bring my darling *zooneleh* for a *bar mitzvah* present?"

As Baby Brother hesitates, Mama breaks in. "Aldous does need a new overcoat."

"Yes, Dad, I can certainly use a new overcoat."

"Okay, that's easy. I got plenty of coats in the store. You can have your pick. What kind would you like?"

Again Aldous hesitates, and Mama says eagerly, "A balmacaan! It should be a balmacaan! With raglan sleeves, you know! And it ought to be a good Scotch tweed!" Carried away as she is (shades of Mr. Rossiter!), Mama is oblivious to the pain that passes across Papa's face and to the strangely pitying look he gives her.

"Yes, Dad, that's exactly what I'd like. A balmacaan in a good Scotch tweed."

Papa frowns. Then after a moment, he sighs and says quietly, "All right, Zooneleh. It just happens I have a balmacaan in your size. A really good coat. A genuine Kuppenheimer."

"Oh, no!" Mama cries. "Everybody knows Brooks Brothers is the best!"

"Yes," echoes Aldous. "Brooks Brothers is what I want."

Papa and I exchange glances. Then he says, "You want a Brooks Brothers? Okay, it'll be a Brooks Brothers."

Mama adds, "Now, Meyer, make sure it has the label."

At that, I can't help laughing. For of course I know what Papa is up to. He has at the store a box containing hundreds of labels of all sorts, some purchased from unscrupulous manufacturers, others removed from various discarded jackets and coats. And the standard comic routine is deciding what kind of label to sew on each suit or coat after it has been patched and repaired and got ready to sell. As he would bite off the last thread and hold the garment up for inspection, Louie the tailor would demand in Yiddish, "Well, what do you think? Maybe Hart Schaffner Marx?"

Jackson would put down the goose and stand back appraisingly: "No, *Genosse* Louie, to me that looks like a Marshall Field. Wouldn't you say so, *Genosse* Alexandra?"

"No, I don't agree with you. I'd say it's more a Chipp's of Cambridge."

Jackson would bow. "The little lady has spoken."

"All right. So it's a Chipp's of Cambridge," Louie would decide. And he would forage in the box for the proper label.

Consequently, when Papa comes home the next evening carrying a cardboard box, I indulge in a conspiratorial smile which makes Christina look at me shrewdly. We all gather around the dining-room table as Papa opens the box and takes out a gray tweed balmacaan with big globular buttons covered in black leather.

Mama at once examines the label, and exclaims, "It's a Brooks Brothers! Oh, Aldous, what a fine coat!"

Papa holds the coat while Aldous gets into it. It is a good fit, and both style and color are right. Aldous prances around the room and pirouettes with pleasure. But there comes the moment when he puts his hand in the pocket, feels something, and brings forth a tuft of pipe-tobacco shreds which he holds out and gazes at, puzzled. Then as he notices the signs of wear at the cuffs and at the buttonholes, puzzlement gives way to realization and chagrin.

Christina laughs unpleasantly. "Brooks Brothers! There's your Brooks Brothers for you, dope! From their well-known secondhand department on the main floor!"

Mama cries out, "Oh, no, Meyer! How could you do that! How *could* you!"

Papa regards her soberly for a minute. "Nellie, what did you think? How would I come to have a brand-new Brooks Brothers coat? Be sensible. It's as fine a coat as you can get. It's a good tweed, a balmacaan, and practically new."

As Aldous, without a word, takes off the

coat and lays it across a chair, Papa sags with sadness. He hasn't meant to be heartless. It has never occurred to him that Aldous and Mama would not really understand that the coat would be secondhand, that they would be so cruelly taken in. Then he heaves a deep sigh: *"Ai, ich hobb a narr fur a veib, un a narr fur a zoon* (I have a fool for a wife, and a fool for a son)." And poor Mama standing there dismayed and poor Aldous trying not to blubber do look like two hopeless hopeless fools. At last Papa tenderly gathers his *zooneleh,* quivering lip and all, into his arms. *"Mein zooneleh!* My darling little *goilem! Ai, mein narrisher narrisher zooneleh!"*

# *Seven*

Even Mr. Rossiter, as neat a knave as he was, might never have made his fatal appeal to Mama's heart, except that it had already been bruised and brayed, worked over with mortar and pestle by Bubbeh. Of course, these two agents, one so necessary to the other, never met, despite their both trampling over the same ground. Indeed, Bubbeh had been dead more than three months before Mr. Rossiter stepped on the scene. I have, in the idle moments that flock to an old maid, tried to fancy a meeting between those two, but my powers have been inadequate. It would be like bringing together two animals from two different geologic eras, or, more precisely, like confronting the fox or otter of reality with a manticore or basilisk out of some dark medieval legend.

Nevertheless, ignorant as Mr. Rossiter was

96

of Bubbeh's prior existence, she did prepare the way for him, as in one of those intricate diseases designed by Universal Providence in which one parasite, through what would seem the most improbable coincidence, must put all in readiness before the second, and otherwise totally unrelated, parasite can do its deadly work. Poor Mama's heart was host in turn to both Bubbeh and Mr. Rossiter. Oh, the tragedy of it! The tragedy of it! However, tragedy requiring a new definition. Not one based on the majestic presence of Fate or Necessity but, rather, one to take account of the commoner chances of human life, such as a crippling illness, an automobile accident, a bank failure, the loss of a job, or, yes, having a parent come to live with you. What is needed is a humbler, more domesticated *Poetics,* a kind of poor man's Aristotle.

Not that Bubbeh, as huge and roughhewn as Papa, and swaddled from the top of her head to the very ground she stood on in voluminous black woolen shawl and skirt, didn't appear (at least to little Lexie) bad-tempered enough, tyrannical and terrifying enough, to be one of the Moirai or Parcae. Like a true fate, she arrived suddenly and unexpectedly on a scene bathed in the light of prosperity. The place was our sunny comfortable house on Phillips, which by then we had come to own outright. The time was perhaps a year after Uncle Avrom was shot, when Papa had taken over the store and was doing very well with it. In response to a letter which his widowed mother back in Poland had had written for her, Papa had sent the money to bring her here. To call the roll of the Davidovs, I was then going on nine, and Christina on five. Papa must have been twenty-six or seven, and Mama thirty. As for Aldous, having not long before this been but a Platonic form waiting out there in the wings, he had just been pumped full of neurotic protoplasm and shoved onstage.

When Bubbeh did make her appearance, no official papers were needed to verify that Papa was her son and that little Lexie was her granddaughter. Neither the transportation to another clime, nor the changes in circumstance, nor the passage of the years had diverted the genes from doggedly reproducing the physical pattern. (The pattern of the soul is something else again.) There were the same heavy bulky body, the Semitic overcast in the complexion, the big fleshy face with its swooping cutlass of a nose. Bubbeh had recently given up the married woman's *sheitel,* or wig, and her own hair, grown out shorter even than Papa's, was clustered on her head in tight iron-gray curls. That masculine cap, together with the black woolen swathings that shrouded any womanly shape, made her seem unsexed, and in a different sense from the ancient Hebraic view of the faithful widow finished with sex and life, and waiting patiently to be translated to a Heaven where she would serve as her husband's compliant *benkeleh.* Bubbeh was no footstool. And there was nothing compliant about her. While it is true that, being then not much past fifty, and allowing for differences in dress, she must have looked much like the Alec of today, it was in a grim version. I do know that Bubbeh was fond of me, and there must have been smiles. Little Lexie often sat on her lap, as Christina never did. Yet in my memory Bubbeh is as likely to smile as is a witch from Macbeth's blasted heath.

*     *     *

Actually, the Bubbeh I see most vividly is the Bubbeh lying in her bed day upon day and week upon week, completely paralyzed after a stroke, or perhaps a series of strokes, had spattered blood on her brain. In all that slack mass only the windows showed life—those intensely black eyes fired by an inner hatred and glaring balefully at everyone who approached. All the rest was inert flesh which had to be fed by means of a tube passing through the nose, heaved on and off the bedpan, and turned this way and that, like an unwieldy sack, to be washed or to have the bed linen changed. Late each afternoon, a practical nurse would come to the house, and she and Mama would disappear into Bubbeh's room, where, behind the door closed against little Lexie, mysterious things went on and mysterious noises could be heard. Of course, as I now realize, the nurse, with Mama's help, must then have administered the catheter, given Bubbeh an enema, and bathed her.

Otherwise, the burden of taking care of that helpless immobile flesh fell upon poor Mama alone. And *that* besides having an infant and two children to care for. Each day for eight long months, she climbed a steep jagged hill of chores and exasperations and loathsome tasks and lacerated feelings, only to have to start at the bottom all over again the next day. As every woman knows, it can be difficult enough to summon up the patience to take care of one you love, with each succeeding sign of weakness making the invalid all the more dear to you. But to have to take care of one whom you hate and fear, whose each new infirmity arouses new resentment, whose death would be a relief devoutly to be wished for, and about whom, moreover, you have a sense of guilt! It is no wonder that Bubbeh lay there like a suppurating abscess in the house. Often enough little Lexie watched Mama (Christina was not allowed in Bubbeh's room) heaving at that slack mass and shedding tears of exhaustion and bitterness while those black malignant eyes glittered at her. And perhaps even then little Lexie understood that, in addition to the never-ending burden, Mama carried deep inside her the torment of what her sick conscience most likely took to be a deserved punishment, a visitation from Heaven, a grinding satisfaction exacted by the sacrament of penance.

Well, at least Bubbeh was bathed frequently and, for the first time in her life, was kept fairly clean. I wonder if that gave Mama any small comfort. For besides everything else so alien in appearance, behavior, and belief, Bubbeh was dirty. And dirty to a degree incredible to a nation and an age given over to the worship of soap and water, mouthwashes and deodorants, underarm daintiness and personal hygiene. Bubbeh's dirt was medieval. It permeated her and pervaded her. It was what you might find in the murkiest alleyways of the Near East. Poor Mama, coming from her well-scrubbed orphanage and regarding cleanliness as more hallowed than godliness, had no preparation for that. Even little Lexie was better prepared, since the world of Papa's store which she frequented was a world of dirt and vermin, of filth, rats, hulking roaches, and green-and-blue jeweled flies, a world where you often came upon a man pissing against the side of a building or behind a wagon in the street. No need for our Dean to shake his head. Even an old-maid schoolteacher may have had her nose rubbed in the muck of life.

Bubbeh brought with her the dirt of the Polish ghetto. Her black woolen shawl and skirt had become a smutched and dusty pelt growing out of her skin. Any embarrassed suggestions by Mama went not only unheeded but uncomprehended, as though made to an aborigine of Africa or Australia. Often when Bubbeh stood in the back yard, she would piss like a mare without self-consciousness, while little Lexie would watch, fascinated, as a pool of urine spread on the ground from under the skirt. And Bubbeh carried a cargo of lice and bedbugs. It was through her that Lexie made the acquaintance of those venerable denizens of the human epidermis. For generally one or the other could be observed creeping along Bubbeh's shawl. I can remember the hysteria with which Mama fought the invasion. The fumes of kerosene still tingle the membrane of my nose as Mama, weeping with dismay, scrubs all the bedsteads and mattresses. And the fine-toothed comb still tugs through my curls as she rubs butter into Christina's and my hair and desperately rakes out the lice.

Mama! Mama darling! Poor poor Mama! Even at this remove of time my heart aches for her. But what of Bubbeh? Ignorant, yes. Superstitious, yes. Dirty and vile-tempered, yes. Yet human. Yet not a monster. With what deep understanding my shrewd Middle Ages erected chapels and cathedrals to *Notre-Dame,* to the Virgin of infinite tenderness, of compassion boundless enough to encompass even a surly God requiring a rainbow to remind him to be merciful! Bubbeh came from the leaden darkness of the ghetto, where the gentiles were not merely the uncircumcised outside the covenant but the execrable enemy who cursed the Jewish presence, spat on the Jewish gabardine, and torched the night with the horrors of the pogrom. She came to a strange land, carrying in her heart a bundle of fears and evil memories, and clutching in her hand a bundle of her most cherished talismans—the seven-branched candelabrum, carved out of solid brass, to be lighted up and prayed before on the Sabbath eve; the bronze *shtossel* to grind nuts or grain in for the holy days; and the mezuzah, with Jehovah's blessing inscribed on the scroll within, to be nailed as protection to the doorpost of the new home. And she came here expecting, in the Oriental manner, to rule in her son's household, with her son's wife a minor official subject to her will.

But after braving the North Sea and the Atlantic and the confusion of Ellis Island, she arrived in the vast unknown city of Cleveland to find her older son Avrom dead, and her younger son without a beard, working like a goy on the Sabbath, eating *trayfehs,* and indifferent to the rites of orthodoxy. In all the ten months spent here before her stroke, she could not bring herself to tolerate the "reformed" ways of the Jews in this land. Mama had to buy Bubbeh dishes, tableware, and pots of her own, so that she could keep *milchiges* and *flayshiges* separated to her satisfaction. Each day she would go off to shop for kosher foods she could trust. Somewhere near Lakeview she hunted out an old-style synagogue with a screened-off section for women which she could attend, though even there she never really lost her misgivings about the orthodoxy of the rabbi. And she was forever in the back yard mumbling incantations and imprecations while she buried a dish or a knife or a spoon to purify it in the earth after some fancied contamination by *trayfehs*.

Worst of all was to find her son Meyer inconceivably wedded to the abhorred gentile. Mama's efforts to ingratiate herself were in vain. Of no avail her speaking Yiddish. Nor her faithfully trying to observe the many rites. She remained a *goyeh*, a species of freak albino lacking a real soul, one of the accursed enemy. But somehow all of Bubbeh's implacable aversion seemed to concentrate itself on Christina, the little blond *goyekeh*, the visible corrupt fruit of the forbidden union. Bubbeh could hardly look at her without muttering and cursing. And unluckily, even at five or six, Christina was not a child to give way or shrink off. Papa rarely saw those two glaring and slapping at each other, since when he came home in the evening it was generally Christina's bedtime. But little Lexie was often an unhappy witness as the huge, swarthy, swaddled grandmother and the defiant, tiny blond granddaughter screamed at each other, each face a rictus of hatred.

Thus it is on that black Friday. I am home from school for lunch. It is a warm, innocent spring day, and down the street can be heard the bell of the bakery wagon. Christina asks Mama for a nickel to buy a cream puff. Bubbeh protests angrily, *"Nayn! Nayn! Es iz trayfehs."* And no doubt those baked goods *are* made with lard, and hence forbidden.

Mama tries to placate her. *"Aber zie iz nur a kind* (But she's only a child!)*"*

All might yet be well, for Bubbeh contents herself with some grumbling. But when Christina comes back into the house, she holds the cream puff up tauntingly to Bubbeh. Mama cries out, "Christina! Stop that! *Christina!"*

The admonition is too late. Infuriated, Bubbeh grabs at the puff, and in the struggle it is mangled and crushed, the lemon-white filling squirting out on Christina's hands and dress. In her rage, Christina beats and kicks at Bubbeh and flings the mashed puff at her. Mama intervenes, but Christina breaks away, runs to the sideboard, and smears the sticky filling from her hands all over Bubbeh's sacred candelabrum.

Bubbeh claps her hand to her cheek and sways her head. *"Oi, gevald! Gottenyoo! Gottenyoo! Morgen iz shabbes!"*

At the moment all Bubbeh is thinking of is that the next day is the Sabbath and the candelabrum must be blessed that evening. She goes out into the kitchen and gets the steaming kettle of water which Mama has put up to boil for the lunch dishes. Surely what Bubbeh intends is to scald the defiled candelabrum in an effort to purify it for use that evening. Just then, however, Christina shrieks something she has heard Lord knows where. *"Alte vershtunkeneh Yiddeneh!* (Stinking old Jewess!)"

Bubbeh's face turns deadly black. *"Ai, du klayne momzer! Du klayne momzer! Ich vell dir gut opbrennen* (You little bastard! You little bastard! I'll give you a good scalding!)"

And she starts for Christina with the kettle of boiling water. Even Christina is frightened, and she runs screeching into the living room and behind the armchair there. Mama throws herself on Bubbeh to hold her back. "Stop! You terrible woman! Stop! What are you doing!"

*"Ich vell die klayne momzer gut opbrennen!"*

Mama pushes Bubbeh so violently that she staggers. "You horrible woman! You must be *insane!* You horrible old woman! *Zoll eich choppen an apoplexy!"* (How sharply I recall that Mama, in wishing a seizure on Bubbeh, still used the respectful second person, not the familiar!)

Bubbeh recovers from that shove, and starts again toward Christina. But there is a sudden change in her gait. For a moment she lurches as if drunk, and then, despite the greatest effort, an effort that brings big drops of sweat to her forehead, can only shuffle a few more steps. The kettle falls from her hand, spilling the hot water across the living-room rug. And then Bubbeh herself slumps to the floor. Mama stands there frozen with horror, while Bubbeh tries desperately to get up, her face swollen and contused, and thick meaningless sounds coming from her mouth.

At last Mama wrings her hands and cries out, "God, I'm cursed! What am I going to do now! God has cursed me!"

And she bends down and strains to lift that mass of inert flesh in her arms. Failing in that, panic-stricken, she starts tugging and lugging and dragging that heavy body toward the davenport. She happens to look up, and she sees me standing there. "Alexandra," she whispers hoarsely, "we must never never tell your father!"

# Eight

Bubbeh gone. *And* Mama gone. The rancor and the narrow fury, the hot tears and the romantic yearnings, all gone. But not forgotten. No, not forgotten. Somewhere, in some gesture, some flicker of thought, some filament of nerve, some cell, some molecule, not forgotten. And nevertheless, gone. Where? How? What? Why? The desperate senseless nagging perpetual questions. The final disintegration of the personality. The diaspora of the elemental atom. Gone into the dark. Into the nothingness. Into the absolute zero of night. Into the no-name-for-it. Into Conrad Aiken's no-time-in-the-heart, no sequence-in-the-brain. Poor foolish Mama, ever one to put the foolish question, would often ask, Where? How? What? Why? And then, with moist lips half parted and eyes gazing dreamily into the vista, would give the rosy-hued answer. If, as Mama would have conjectured in one of her poetical, sadly smiling moods, roses, red roses have sprung from her flesh, then what from Bubbeh's? No doubt some species of thorny, spiny, hairy cactus. And from the handsome Mr. Alan Rossiter's? An elegant meat-eating orchid. But more often than flowery poetical, Mama was misty religious. Then, like those ubiquitous women kneeling on the church pavement, shuffling their beads and kissing the sacred image, Mama would construct out of the sleazy fabric of her wishes "another world," "another life."

"Alexandra," she would say to me during those last months when we were so much together, "after I am gone, let there be no tears and no wearing of black. I don't want you to waste your precious days mourning for me."

"Your obedient daughter promises nothing, Mama."

She would disregard my levity. "No, don't you grieve for me, Alexandra. There is really no need to. I'm sure we're going to meet again elsewhere—in another world—where we'll find all our loved ones, all those who were once dear to us."

At times, Papa's *tochterl* would demand impatiently, "What world, Mama? Where is it, that other world you keep talking about? Let me have its location, if you please, the crossing of latitude and longitude that marks its place."

And Mama would declare with a knowing smile, "Oh, it's there! You'll see! Another world! Another life! You'll see it all in God's good time, Alexandra." Then, reading Papa's skepticism darkly mirrored in my Jewish face, she would add, "You don't believe me, do you?"

"No, Mama. No matter how much you cry, they don't give you back your marbles. The play is for keeps. And when it's over, it's over."

"You think you know it all, don't you, just because you're a college professor and have read a lot of books."

"Not because I'm a college professor, Mama. Because I'm Meyer Davidov's daughter and a Jew. A mocking, sardonic unbeliever of a Jew." Then, of course, I would instantly regret my harshness. "But Mama darling, I grant you I may be wrong. I hope for your sake I am wrong."

And I *do* hope against hope (ah, there at last it is, *das ewig Weibliche*) that I am dead wrong, and that Mama has entered expectantly upon "another world" and "another life," somewhere beyond the chemistry of the grave, on the farther side of the spongy bone and the bloated, grinning coffin worm. And I hope that Bubbeh, too, has found her Heaven, where she can forever mumble before her consecrated seven-branched candelabrum and prostrate herself as her husband's faithful *benkeleh*.

Poor foolish Mama. Waiting with childish trust, on a promissory note secured by worthless collateral, for "another world," "another life," she allowed *this* life to slip, or rather drag, by. But "allowed" is not the precise word. For she was like a person who endures some long-drawn-out trial supported only by the expectation of the relief or the reward at the distant end. At any rate, after Bubbeh, having lain paralyzed for eight long months, slowly, slowly, finally expired, and after the sensation of deliverance, and after the brief romantic interlude with Mr. Rossiter, Mama settled down to mere existence, to marginal subsistence, to a kind of waiting it out on this sterile promontory the earth.

The stifled desperation revealed itself in the way she ate. It was not the nibbling out of boredom or nervousness which so many of my spinster colleagues indulge in. Nor was it the eating with gusto and smacking of the lips to be observed in Papa and, I must confess, in Papa's *tochterl*. No, it was compulsive. To put a crudeness crudely, Mama stuffed her mouth. Like an alcoholic with liquor, she was unable to stop as long as there was any food within reach. A pitiful illness, yes. But there was something decidedly unpleasant about the sight of Mama at the table, not so much eating as driven to eat, chomping and swallowing without discrimination the *disjecta membra* of fish, flesh, or fowl, the cold mashed potatoes, the odds and ends of side dishes, the remains of the pastry, chomping away until everything edible was lost to view down her gullet. Of course, she quickly put on fat—indeed, sank herself in it—and the slender good-looking blonde of the cracked and yellowed photo which I treasure disappeared. It was as though she had deliberately gone into hiding. And in her stead appeared the Mama

Christina and Aldous knew, the obese Mama of the coarsened, darkened hair, the heavy face and gross humped neck, the thick torso riding on the absurdly thin legs. The earlier girlish Mama submerged herself, to emerge thirty years later as the sick, frail, feeble old woman querulously waiting for the end.

And in my memory each Mama has her habitat. The earlier Mama dwells happily, humming or singing to herself, in the house on Phillips. Whereas the usurper, the plump corseted body, belongs to Fairport Avenue. It belongs to the period when the visible tokens of the Davidov prosperity grew steadily shabbier, when the household goods as they wore out were not repaired or replaced, when no effort was made to keep up. The mainspring had snapped. Mama just seemed to let go. Oh, she performed the tasks expected of her, but without taking pleasure in the doing or in the accomplishment. Thus she continued to cook Papa's favorite dishes, although, with the heart gone out of her, they were not quite up to their former excellence, and Papa would complain that the horse-radish relish was not sharp enough or that the

117

stuffed *kishka* was too dry or that the strudel was soggy.

And apparently she continued another function (it must have been so one-sided as to constitute rape). For this was the period when Mama would come staggering home from a mysterious morning visit and take to her bed for the afternoon, sick and faint, gripped by fits of dizziness and vomiting. Christina was then too young, even for Christina, to comprehend, but Lexie, her intuition ground to a fine edge by all the zigzags in the family fortunes, quickly guessed at the aborticides. And this was the period when friends began to fall away. Perhaps, having moved onto the Heights, then the goal of Cleveland's successful middle-class Jews, they were embarrassed by the Davidov decline. Or, it may be, they sensed that Meyer and Eleanor Davidov had become self-destroyers pursued and torn apart by ravening hounds in a Dantean wood of their own making.

Certainly that rage to destroy themselves lay naked in their gambling. For it was after the move to Fairport that both Papa and Mama fell into card playing (mostly poker), but not as a game so much as a miasmal fever. Papa was a reckless player. But Mama was absurd, pathetically so. She never really caught on to the game, and she lacked the quick wit and the quick decision needed for it. Most men wouldn't have played with her, for she was so poor a player she spoiled the game. But women are heartless in gambling. And "the girls" played with Mama only to fleece her. Which inhumane feat they accomplished with sickening regularity.

Mama played without pleasure, her face mostly sullen, her eyes glazed, stupefied as though by a narcotic, impatiently looking at each card as it was dealt to her, just waiting for the next card, for the next hand, for the next game, for the—there!—there!—*there!*—it would come, it would unfold, it would *be!* Often enough Lexie was able to look on, when she came home from school to find "the girls" assembled for an afternoon of nickel-and-dime poker. By then poor Mama would be at the stage of trying frantically, and so obviously in vain, to get even, to win back a little of the housekeeping money she had already lost. She would be staying in with every hand, with laughably impossible hands—when it was draw poker, with three cards to a flush, or three cards to a straight; when it was stud, against a pair of aces showing, or without a single face card. Of course, Mama never won. For even when fantastic luck came her way, her excited face would betray her and she wouldn't know how to make the most of her hand.

With Papa and Mama both losing so heavily at cards, no wonder the money drained away and the Davidovs were so often in need. No wonder Papa had at last to sell the store and find himself a job working for someone else. No wonder, also, there were so many bitter quarrels. To take Papa's side for a moment, it was not that Mama always lost. I'm sure that Papa didn't mind her losing, although he was well aware of how absurd a player she was. It was that she never told the truth about her losses, and her evasions and lies infuriated him.

"Well, Nellie," he would ask good-humoredly, "how did you make out with your girls this afternoon?"

Invariably Mama would send forth her little counterfeit laugh. "My *girls!* What an expression to use! For silly middle-aged women with nothing better to do than play cards!"

"Okay, with your silly middle-aged women with nothing better to do than play cards. How did the game go?"

"*Game!* You could hardly call it a game."

Papa would insist, "Okay, so it wasn't a game. But you played *something* all afternoon! Did you win or lose?"

"Oh, I must have won a few cents, I suppose. It was so little either way I can't really be sure. Anyhow, it was nothing worth talking about." (And I, having looked on, would *know* that Mama had lost at least ten or twenty dollars.)

Then, later in the evening, having, as she thought, given Papa time to forget, she would say, "Meyer, I need seven dollars to pay the gas bill tomorrow."

Papa would frown. "But Nellie, I thought you said you paid that last week."

"Oh, I was going to tell you. I couldn't pay

it after all. We still owed ten dollars on the rent."

"You mean you didn't pay the landlord all the rent on the first of the month?"

"Meyer, I can't come running to you for every penny. I had to use part of the rent money to pay the butcher. Last month I had to charge a lot of things with him. You remember we had the Zabludovs and the Silvermans and the Bernsteins over for dinner. I had to buy an extra chicken to roast. And whitefish has gone up so. I'd change butchers, only this one does give us credit when we need it."

And as Mama would go on, adding to the tangle of circumstantial detail and *non sequiturs,* Papa's face would get blacker and blacker.

Through either precocious prudence or childish unconcern, Christina and Aldous would stay well outside these quarrels, and wait for the storm to blow over. But Lexie would hover on the outskirts, intervening when she could, trying with adolescent earnestness to remodel her parents. Her efforts came to an abrupt and ignominious end one evening. Lexie was then fifteen, already nearly the size of the Alec of today, but as yet an adult in cubic measure only. The usual quarrel between Papa and Mama had almost run its course when she began to exhort them, "But Mama, Papa, we ought to save *something!* Don't you see it isn't right to live always on the edge the way we do? Papa's store brings in a good income. Then why are we always so broke? Every family I know puts *some* money aside each week, to buy a car or a refrigerator or a house. Or just for a rainy day. Why can't *we?*"

Mama said firmly, "Now Alexandra, you're just a child and you shouldn't mix into things that don't concern you or you don't understand."

"I'm *not* a child, Mama. I'm fifteen years old. These things do concern me. I *am* part of the family, you know. And what I don't understand is how so much money can slip away with nothing to show for it."

Mama was provoked. "One day you'll have a family of your own and you'll be able to run it your own way. Maybe then you'll realize how much money it takes to keep up a home and raise three children. And that's not all. We have so many debts!"

"Why *are* we always in debt?" Lexie unluckily persisted. And then, in her girlish zeal she asked the question she had never thought (or dared?) to ask before: "Where did all the money go when we sold the house on Phillips?"

Papa and Mama both flinched, as if flicked with a whip. The blood drained out of Mama's face, and Papa's swarthy skin took on a yellowish cast. But Lexie failed to notice the ominous silence, and went on with blind eagerness, "Mama, Papa, why don't you let me put aside just ten dollars a week? You won't miss it. And at the end of a year we'll have five hundred dollars in the bank. In two years it'll be a *thousand* dollars! Or even *five* dollars a week to start with. Just pretend you don't have it. Pretend you lost it at cards. Pretend it was stolen from you. Pretend *anything!* Pretend you gave it away to charity. Or pretend someone cheated you out of it. Pretend—"

That was when Papa leaned over the table and slapped me across the cheek as hard as he could. I can still feel the sting. Even Christina gasped. My head was jarred and my jaw fell open. But greater than the physical pain was the shock. That was the only time in my life Papa struck me. I looked into his eyes, and instantly looked away. Of course, I forgave him. For I could not say, with Desdemona, "I have not deserved this."

*Nine*

To finish this story, there remain only the letters and reliques still tied in the pink satin ribbon now soiled and frayed by time. Perhaps a Henry Adams, always searching for relations and hidden links, would have seen the connection between that little packet and the slap across the face Papa had given Lexie three decades ago. However, Alec was simply confounded. She had not so much as guessed at the existence of the little sentimental packet. To think that for so many years Mama had cherished it! Where had she kept it all that time? And had Papa known about it? *There* was the extra turn of the screw.

Well, Alec certainly had plenty to brood about as she drove with Papa on a recent afternoon the length of Superior, across the High-Level Bridge and then south along West

Twenty-fifth Street and Pearl Road almost to Parma. And later, too, as she stood with Papa at Mama's grave and studied the newly incised headstone, noting the place reserved for herself to spend eternity in (or, rather, not to exaggerate, just the five billion years still left before the Sun flickers out, the Earth grows cold, and Man disappears) and noting also that several citizens had taken up residence in the little unkempt graveyard since Mama's funeral nearly a year before. And, above all, as she inhaled the odor of the roses, the red roses which Papa, not Alec, had thought of stopping to buy.

But to go back. It was nearly two o'clock on that afternoon when I drove up Lakeview, turned east on Fairport, and parked in front of the old familiar house. Somehow everything about it sagged. Not one straight line had survived. The gnarled, contorted oak, only half clothed in the rags of leaves, still crowded the scrap of front lawn; the clumps of plantain were still there, muddy now from some recent rains; the blistered and rusted iron railing was more sway-backed than ever. After Mama's death, Papa had stayed on, partly because of inertia, it is true, but more, I now realize, because of the toughness of the ligament binding him to Mama. (How his present lostness, his need for her, would have warmed poor Mama's romantic heart!) I had engaged Mrs. Gastineau to come in each day to make up the bed, dust around a bit, and look after things, but Papa ate all his meals out, condemned to a vain search for those favorite foods Mama had once prepared for him.

Climbing the crooked steps to the front porch, I entered the door to the living room and called, "Papa!" There was no reply. I wondered at that, since he was to have asked for the afternoon off. (Even after the many years, it was hard to think of Papa not having his own store, working for someone else, not being his own boss.) I walked slowly through the rooms. All the old familiar furniture was still there to greet me, including the ancient upright piano and Baby Brother's drooping davenport. But everything was shabbier than ever, and yet at the same time had an air of being unused, like a small neglected parlor off the lobby of a cheap hotel. Even the refrigerator in the kitchen was empty, except for half-a-dozen cans of beer. In Mama's room, to which Papa had moved after her death, the bed was made up, but the pillows were newly rumpled. Papa must have rested there a while. The only other sign of habitation was at Papa's place at the head of the dining-room table, where a punctured beer can, a glass stained with stale froth, and a chipped saucer of cigarette ashes and stubs showed he had recently been sitting. That little still-life saddened me. It gave off the brooding loneliness of an Edward Hopper painting.

By chance, I happened to look at the sideboard and saw that the bottom drawer was pulled open a little. As I went to shut it, I found there the unexpected little packet. Tied in the soiled pink satin ribbon were some folded theater programs, some stiff parchmentlike official or commercial papers, and three letters still in their envelopes. I saw that the uppermost envelope was addressed in Mama's schoolmarmish handwriting, in a faded lavender ink that must once have been deep purple: "Mr. Alan Rossiter, Wade Park Hotel, Euclid Avenue, Cleveland, Ohio." Underneath, someone had scribbled in pencil, now blurred and smudged, "No forwarding address." I went out on the porch and sat in the swing. I knew that Papa must be at the joint around the corner on Lakeview and would be back soon. The little packet lay unopened in my lap. Despite my curiosity, I found myself reluctant to undo the ribbon, and I simply gazed into space.

It was a fine day. The warmth of late September had once more dulcified the air after the recent rains. White puffballs of cloud hung like ripe fruit in the brilliant-blue sky. A few fallen oak leaves adhered to the sidewalk and curb in ragged brown patches. With most of the children away at school, it was unusually quiet. The street actually looked pleasant and inviting. Even though Papa's house had deteriorated steadily from visit to visit, the neighborhood as a whole, I noticed, was showing signs of improvement as more and more Negroes bought homes for themselves. It was easy to pick out those houses occupied by their proud owners. They were clean and in good repair, freshly painted, with trim lawns and an occasional flower bed displaying the faded yellow, gold, orange, and rust of chrysanthemums and zinnias. I filled my lungs with the sweet air. Yes, it was a beautiful day, a day expressly created for the refreshment of spirit and mind. But it failed to dispel the weight on my heart.

I tried to persuade myself that what dejected me was knowing Papa had descended to the beer joint on Lakeview. I had been there once with him, and it had given me the willies. Manny's, whatever Aldous felt about it, was at least alive, filled with noise and light. But this beer joint around the corner (it didn't even have a *name*) was a dead and putrid thing. Like some marine parasite, it occupied the abandoned shell of a sorry little grocery, the grimy walls scarred where the shelves and other fixtures had been ripped away. The interior was dirty, dark, stale. The original counter, with the addition of a spigot and a zinc tub to rinse glasses in, now served as the bar. Behind it officiated the owner, a surly Negro woman in a slatternly dress, who had only a beer license but who would surreptitiously (for a price, of course) pour you a slug of raw whiskey out of a bottle which she kept hidden in an old beer carton. The few patrons were the refuse of the neighborhood. They were first cousins to the objects you see floating in a pool of stagnant water.

No, that beer joint was not at all the right setting for Papa, and it hurt me to think of him there. I was tempted to ask him once more to throw up his job and come to share my apartment. However, I hesitated. He did need his job, and not for the money alone. Nor could he really be expected to flourish transplanted to my decorous college town with its three thousand prim citizens. It was a fine and private place to read a good book in. But whom would Papa seek out for companionship? One of my spinster colleagues? Our dear Dean? Where would he find his vital noise and light? And his poker games? And his Manny's? Or even a dismal sour-smelling beer joint? As for his going to live with his other children—there were certainly joints aplenty in New York, but it was impossible to picture Papa and Aldous lodged together among those neatly placed vases and books. Even if Zooneleh could in all reason be called upon to harbor the very enemy he had taken refuge from. And no doubt there was a sufficiency of beer in Milwaukee, but Papa and Tom Frederick had never been comfortable with each other. Even if an invitation had been forthcoming from Christina.

But, of course, there was still another reason why Papa would not—no, *could not*—leave the house where Mama had died. The bond, though not so material and visible as that frayed pink satin ribbon in my lap, was not to be broken, nor loosened. No matter how desperately Papa wandered from bar to bar, the house was the magnetic center that pulled him back. Half a century of dwelling in a common matrix of affection and hatred, passion and boredom, habit and revolt, reality and dream, had clasped, clamped, and riveted Papa and Mama together. They were an amalgam, a fusion, mortise and tenon, hook and eye, hub and wheel. They were the bush and the vine that die as one.

We come to those letters. Ah, those letters, those letters! Can it be that all love letters are so banal? That question the old-maid school-teacher cannot answer, having yet to write or to receive her first love letter. I speak only of actual love letters, not those many published items, obviously literary efforts from the start, created with the writer's artistic ego standing at his shoulder and applauding each elegant phrase. But poor Mama! Poor foolish foolish Mama! Could she help it that those cries from her innermost self came forth garbed in the shoddiest stereotypes, stale platitudes lingering in the recesses of her mind from her girlhood reading in *Graustark, When Knighthood Was in Flower,* and *To Have and To Hold?* Poor Mama's genuine emotion transpired in a shadow language. And in a prim schoolmarmish hand, all proper in grammar, punctuation, and spelling. Poor Mama. But "poor Mama" not because of the clichés she used. It is rather that she wrote thus to one unworthy, to one indeed nonexistent, to a mere romantic apparition. Well, as I sometimes say when I grow impatient with all my pedantic backing and filling, "Miss Alexandra, ma'am, let us without further ado!"

*Monday evening*

Dearest Alan,

Oh, where were you this afternoon? I waited for nearly two hours until I was forced to hurry home before my husband returned. I went back and forth between the indoor garden at the Museum and our bench beside the little lake out in front, thinking perhaps I had misunderstood or misremembered where we were to meet. Two hours, Alan! Each made up of sixty long minutes, each minute of sixty long seconds! You cannot imagine my feeling, with what fever of hope and anxiety I listened for your footstep. You are not a woman. You cannot know how for her, love is all in all. Now I am distraught with worry and fear. What has happened? Are you ill? Has there been some accident? Were you prevented by some unexpected business? Or has my poor mind got confused as to where and when we were to meet? You will think me immodest to pour out my heart on paper this way. I never believed that I, Eleanor Davidov, a respectable married woman, would come to this. I keep asking myself over and over, Can this be I? Can this be I? Never before did I do anything to tarnish my name. But I am sure I can trust you and the trust will not be misplaced. As I sit here and look into the night for my thoughts, I realize that we must have been fated to meet. Otherwise, how account for the unbelievable chance that brought two total strangers together at Wade Park? Out of all the days in the year, that one day! Out of all the hours in the day, that one hour! Out of all the places on this vast globe, that one place! Except that we were really not strangers. As soon as you made so bold as to speak to me, I felt that I knew you. Your very voice told me you were different from all other men. Tomorrow afternoon at four I'll be at the same place, and every afternoon till you come again. I say no more, but be there, be there! Do not disappoint me!

*Your Eleanor*

*Wednesday evening*

*Dearest Alan,*

I am alarmed. Three days now, without a sign of you. Yesterday and again this afternoon I waited and waited, each moment an eternity.

And I hurried back and forth from one place to another like a madwoman. I almost went to the desk clerk at your hotel to inquire after you. I did get as far as the doors. But I was afraid of what they might think. You once said to me— you have probably forgotten, but the words are engraved in my memory—you said I have the heart of a young girl. That is true, even though to all outward appearance I am a married woman with a husband and three children. I feel so strangely awkward and inexperienced beside you. You awakened me through love. My way was narrow and dark and beset with thorns. I had not met with much true love or courtesy or compassion in my life. My marriage had no real romance in it. Then you came to the rescue like young Lochinvar. Can I ever forget that day? The moment we met I said to myself, He's so handsome and he has such fine manners, he's a real gentleman. Meeting with you repaid me for years of hopeless waiting. The winter was over. The trees were green and the flowers were in bloom. The sunshine was a flood of pure gold. The birds sang in my heart. I will not believe that our spring will not have a summer. I remember the first time you kissed me, I covered my face with my hands. Thereafter I walked in a dream. I saw only your face, heard only your voice. It was a beautiful dream from which one fears no wakening. Oh, tell me God will be good to me! If only I can be near you! Tell me we shall be happy once more. Tomorrow I shall wait at the same place. I beseech and implore you! Do not fail me!

*Your Eleanor*

*Thursday evening*

*Dearest beloved Alan,*

Oh, I shall go mad, I shall go mad! Again you were not there. I keep asking myself, What has happened to him? If you fail me tomorrow, I shall throw aside all decency and inquire at the desk of your hotel. It no longer matters what they will think. I see I am a woman without shame. And yet I can't help feeling that I am innocent within and have done no wrong. Oh, despise me if you will! I lay everything bare. You *must* take me away with you. Shall I plead with you? I am ready to. Shall I beg on my knees? Shall I come crawling to you in the dirt? I am ready to. I am abject. I am ready to leave behind all that a woman holds dear. Say but "come" and I will come. Life is so short, so short. There is only the one life. What if it gets off wrong? Is there to be no way of setting it straight? No deliverance? I can't believe God means it to be so. Before you came, I existed in a dungeon. I beat against the walls. But there was no way out. Was I ever to live again? It seemed not. Then you came and brought a message of hope. You came as if to take me home. That afternoon when we first met I was sitting beside the little lake in Wade Park looking for nothing but rest and peace and quiet dreaming. It was like returning from a voyage with an un-expected precious cargo. I walked hand in hand with the sweetness of true love. Yes, yes, yes, yes, we were meant for each other. We belong to each other. Only speak the word! Tell me it is not just a vain dream, it shall be a reality. With all my heart I love you, oh, my lover, oh, my be-loved! I will always love you, and you alone. Have pity on me. Listen kindly, look into your heart, and have pity on me. I am a woman, weak and helpless. As you are my sword and my shield, be there tomorrow! As you hold me dear, keep this tryst!

*Your Eleanor*

# *Ten*

It was, I suppose, the creaking of the porch swing, as much as the letters and other reliques in my lap, that carried me back to the time just before Mr. Rossiter, the fatal Mr. Alan Rossiter, appeared on the scene. Actually, I was not listening to this swing, covered in a rainproof figured drill and rocking in its metal cradle, but to that other swing where Papa and Mama had been wont to sit, that old-fashioned swing with seat and back made of wood slats and suspended by iron links from bolts in the ceiling. I thought again of that house on Phillips where Bubbeh had lain paralyzed for eight interminable months, draining Mama of vital spirits and converting her into the shuck that a spider hangs out on its web. I thought of that December when Bubbeh had at long last died and the tending of that slack mass had come to an end. All through January, February, and March, Mama crept about in a stupor of exhaustion. Although only thirty-two years old, she had passed out of the landscape of youth and into that of middle age. Her slender rounded figure had become bony and angular, her face pinched, her throat and neck stringy. She had no resiliency. Despite her thinness, she moved heavily, giving off no sense of relief or release. She must have been on the edge of a breakdown.

Not until April was there a change. It may have been spring's awakening, the sight of the new-uplifted tulips and daffodils bordering the lawn and of the earliest buds swelling on Mama's beloved lilac bushes, the prevailing texture of the weather. A restlessness invaded Mama, and she would roam without purpose through the house, and then sit out on the porch swing, staring into space and letting the housework go undone. Above all, she seemed to *need* to be outdoors. She craved the open air. And with three children to take care of (I was ten, Christina six, and Aldous two), she *was* a prisoner. Often when Christina and I came home from school, Mama would leave Aldous with an obliging neighbor, and take us with her for a rambling walk along the parkway on Thornhill Drive, or even for an aimless streetcar ride. There was a kind of desperation in these excursions. One afternoon she took us to the foot of Gordon Park, where she simply sat on a ledge and looked quietly out at the glittering expanse of Lake Erie and at the waves breaking into spume on the rocky shore.

But her favorite place came to be Wade Park and the Art Museum. It may have been during our spring vacation. At any rate, I recall that for a while we went there day after day. Mama would sit in the subdued olive light of the Museum's indoor garden amid the antique statuary, her back erect, her hands folded in her lap, her eyes vacantly focused on the small rectangular pool of water, while Christina and I explored the armor hall with the arrays of curiously shaped swords and daggers, or the Egyptian room with the mummy cases and the terracotta figurines in the tiny mortuary boats. Or Mama would sit for a couple of hours at a stretch out in front of the Museum, on one of the benches alongside the little artificial lake where the swans floated gracefully and serenely.

All these memorabilia are not to moan the expense of many a vanished sight. No, it is rather that a sense of Mama's morbid restlessness and inexpressible longing at that time may help to understand what followed. Yet perhaps these explanations, like all explanations of human behavior, are beside the point. Perhaps the readiness was all. One such afternoon, Christina and I had been playing on the far side of the little lake, trying in vain to attract the swans by calling and beckoning to them, and we returned to find a strange man sitting on the bench and talking to Mama. The curtain had gone up without our witnessing it, and the play had already advanced beyond the opening exposition. Even ten-year-old Lexie could observe that Mama was fluttering and that red stains burned in her cheeks.

Mama tugged at our dresses to straighten them, and then presented us. "Alexandra. Christina. Now show your good manners and say 'How do you do?' to Mr. Rossiter. Mr. Rossiter has just come to our city of Cleveland. He means to settle down if he likes it here. But for the time he is staying just over there at the hotel."

"Alexandra," the man said with a smile after we had mumbled our how-do-you-do's, "you are a braw bonny lassie. And Christina, what a wee pretty miss. But truly now, Mrs. Davidov, these can nae be your daughters. You are much too young a woman for that. These must be your wee sisters."

"Mr. Rossiter, you must not flatter me."

"Nae, nae, Mrs. Davidov. I don't mean to flatter. I am not that kind of man. But seriously, I hope ye ken ye are a verra fortunate woman, to have two such bonny daughters."

Clearly Mama had already taken to Mr. Rossiter. Christina also took to him quickly and was soon perched on his lap, even though now she does not, I am certain, so much as recall his existence, having been too young then for memory to sink its fangs in her. As for little Lexie, she stared at the man fascinated. It was not only that he was a gentile of a sort she had never seen around Papa's store. Nor was it only the theatrical burr and the Scotticisms—probably the bogus fabrication of my memory. In Papa's circle, verbal gallantry was unknown, and Lexie had never heard a man talk in such a manner. Moreover, Mr. Rossiter looked different from the men she knew, and dressed differently. It is strange how his image fixed itself in Lexie's mind. He looked trim, and he had finish. He was a man of about forty (I guess at that), slender, slightly taller than Mama, with a clipped, sandy mustache, a nose almost pug, and light-blue eyes. He had an agreeable face and an assured air. His clothes, as Lexie could even then judge from her experience at Papa's store, were expensive, including such rare elegance as cuff links. I don't know how he dressed for the evening, since I never saw him then. But for the afternoon he wore a lightweight balmacaan in a brownish tweed, a brown felt hat, and dark-brown oxfords of a thick leather with a dull gloss. Above all, he never failed to be soft-spoken and courteous.

Now, of course, given all her wisdom, Alexandra wonders at how Mama (or, I am sure, the countless other women) could have been taken in by so spurious an article. But then, people who don't live in glass houses shouldn't throw stones. Certainly Alexandra is in no position to pass judgment. Her virtue is, alas, a blank virtue, having never been tried. Mama, whatever else is to be said about her, was out in the real market place where woman sells the commodity the Wife of Bath calls her "beste quoniam."

The next afternoon Mama again took Christina and Lexie to the little artificial lake in front of the Art Museum, and again Mr. Rossiter appeared on the scene. Was it all by pre-arrangement? Had he left some parting suggestion? Or did poor foolish Mama just return there hopefully? Little Lexie couldn't tell. Just as she couldn't follow each step in Mr. Rossiter's wooing of Mama. On the afternoon following that, he showed up again, this time stepping out of a sleek maroon sports roadster. And he took Mama, together with Christina and Lexie, for a drive down the winding road through Rockefeller Park and along the lake front east to Bratenahl, where Cleveland's princes of commerce and industry had their *palazzi.*

At least Alexandra now *thinks* she remembers that drive. Through her mind flash the sharp disjunct images—Mama and the two little girls crowded in the seat of the elegant roadster with Mr. Rossiter, the unfamiliar road winding through the greenery of Rockefeller Park and through the dark tunnels under the streets passing overhead, the brilliant glimpses of Lake Erie and the brisk wind blowing their hair, the fabulous mansions of Bratenahl set behind groves of trees or surrounded by wonderful flower gardens and spacious lawns. However, those images exist only in the fun house of memory, a place of trick mirrors, bewildering mazes and blind alleys, trap doors and wobbly floors, and lifelike wax figures appearing momentarily in sudden alternations of colored dark and colored light. Of one thing I feel pretty sure. It was during that drive that Lexie several times heard Mr. Rossiter call Mama not Mrs. Davidov but Eleanor, rounding off the "r" with a fine roll.

After that drive, little Lexie never again actually saw Mr. Rossiter. But she knew he was there. Oh, she knew he was there. Mama took to leaving both Aldous and Christina at home for an hour or two in charge of Lexie, while she went off alone. Lexie had no doubt it was to meet Mr. Rossiter. Where did they go? What did they do? How did they spend the time? Questions that cannot be answered, except in the tinsel and paste of fiction. At the far end of four decades, Mama and Mr. Rossiter are two strangers standing together on a station platform seen from a train passing by. What, after all, do I really know of *that* Mama? To Alec, she always seemed prim, proper, prudish. And yet, she had at least once before been seduced, to use a quaint old-fashioned term for a quaint old-fashioned act. I mean by Papa.

Certainly the sequence of events is blurred. There did come a Saturday when Lexie, on the pretext that Mama was going to take her to see an exhibit at the Art Museum, failed to accompany Papa to the store. Instead, she stayed at home to look after Aldous and Christina for the afternoon, while Mama went with Mr. Rossiter to see *Rose Marie* at the Hanna. For this my memory does have the corroborating evidence of those theater programs treasured for so many years. What an occasion that must have been for Mama, who had probably never before seen a real live musical show. I recall that she wore her very best dress, a dark-blue crepe with shirring at the waist, and that Mr. Rossiter bought her a corsage of gardenias, which she kept thereafter in her dresser drawer. As I can now tell from the theater programs, there were at least two other such matinees with Mr. Rossiter—to see *The Student Prince* and *The Desert Song*.

Well, there could be no doubt that all through April, May, and June Mama lived in a fever of anticipation and excitement. She was transformed. While she was still thin, the angularity and the pinched look were gone. She appeared younger, more beautiful. And she no longer moved heavily. Why didn't Papa notice the change in her? And why didn't he guess at what was going on? Or did he? Perhaps not, since he was away at the store until evening, and Mama was always back in time to prepare dinner and pick up the routine of the house. And who, after all, was to sound the tocsin? Not the infant Aldous. Not six-year-old Christina. Not even Papa's *tochterl*, who so readily fell in with Mama's secrecy. Mr. Rossiter once sent home a big heart-shaped satin-covered box of expensive chocolates to repay Lexie for taking care of Aldous and Christina. But that bribe wasn't necessary. No bribe was needed to make an accessory of little Lexie.

Now and again Mama would prompt her, "Alexandra, we won't say anything to your father about this afternoon. I had some shopping to do downtown, and I want it to be a surprise to him."

The suggestion was superfluous. In a way, how reckless it was of Mama to put herself thus at the mercy of a girl of ten! Or was it just that she knew her little Lexie?

While I sat on the swing, pondering on that little Lexie of long ago and on how much she herself had understood of what lay coiled in her bosom, I saw Papa come around the corner from Lakeview and walk slowly along Fairport toward the house. In the early afternoon sun, his hair, though thick and curly as ever, was now *gray*. Yes, Papa had aged in the year since Mama's death. And there was no spring to his walk. Nevertheless, he was still an imposing man, with his great bulk and his massive chest and shoulders. And the roughhewn head and face were still impressive. Even the nose, although its cutting edge was now dulled by fat, remained quite a weapon. At a distance Papa became aware of me, and he waved. I was about to go to meet him. But before I could get up from the swing, a figure detached itself from me. And suddenly little Lexie was there, running to meet Papa on Phillips and to dip her hand into his coat pocket for the chocolate bar or the bag of gumdrops, all the time guiltily keeping her secret about Mama and Mr. Rossiter. Ah, perfidious little Lexie! Just look at her run to Papa! The little cheat! Just look at her! The little traitress! *The little bawd!*

# Eleven

What rubbed the magic lamp and summoned up the marionettes from the thick air of memory was the sheaf of glossy parchmentlike papers. While Papa was plodding along Fairport toward the house, I unfolded those papers to have a quick look at them. On the instant, I recalled having seen them before. There were six sheets, each signifying a thousand shares in His Imperial Majesty's Royal Klondike Mines. Even in appearance, the stock was phony. The name of the company swirled across the top in a parabola of Gothic type stamped in gold. Beneath that was a long statement about the location and prospects of the mines, printed in boldface, still the original deep, confident blue. In the lower left-hand corner was an elaborate gold seal, and in the lower right-hand corner were three signatures, illegible because of the curlicues, purporting to be those of the officers of the company. The stiff ivory-colored paper was shot through with threads and flecks of gold. That stock crackling in my hands brought back a strange night across almost four decades of time, a night flecked with strange colors and sounds, and threaded with lights, half-lights, and shadows.

The scene is our house on Phillips, with the windows and the front door wide open, so that the indoors is invaded by the outdoors and the electric lights mingle with the night. It is close to the Fourth of July, perhaps even the Fourth itself, and little Lexie's head bangs with the firecrackers and blazes with the pinwheels and Roman candles. It is during that pre-safe-and-sane era, when the Fourth fills each neighborhood for days with fiery lozenges and stars and flowers, disks and wheels and spirals, arrows and crescents and spangles, all in rose, peach, amber, violet, saffron, amethyst, indigo, jade, and every wonderful dye, lighting up the trees and bushes, flaring up against the leaves, shining in through the open doors and windows. All this sputtering of color casts an unreal lighting upon the scene, and each actor on stage is jarred apart, scattered like the lights, limned in glowing neon pigments. No wonder that strange night seems a hallucination, and Alexandra now cannot be sure which of the events are actual, which are served up by imagination or juggled by memory.

It is Friday evening, and Papa has come home from the store in good time for his favorite meal of the week. But—most unusual—Mama is not there, and he finds not the slightest sign of preparation. The candles on the sideboard are not lit, nor are the *challehs* ranged on the clean white cloth, their varnished russet surfaces reflecting the candlelight. There is no *gefillte* fish on the table, no plate of *knaydlach* and stuffed *helzl,* no aroma of roast chicken pervading the house. Instead, he comes home to find ten-year-old Lexie in charge of an unruly Christina and an Aldous crying because he needs to be changed.

Papa asks, "Lexie darling, where's Mama?"

"I don't know, Papa. She went away about four o'clock. She didn't say where she was going. But she told me not to worry, you would be home soon."

If Papa is troubled, he covers up well. "I see. You children have had nothing to eat?"

"No, Papa."

Papa takes hold with surprising efficiency. He sends Lexie out to the delicatessen on 123rd Street, and by the time she comes running back with the lox and corned beef and pastrami, the rye bread and strudel and milk, Papa has subdued Christina and changed Aldous. Lexie gets the table set and the meal served. It makes an extraordinary dinner for Friday night, and certainly an odd meal for us children. But we find an excitement in it. And after it is finished, Lexie clears the table and washes the dishes, while Papa puts Christina and Aldous to bed. By then it must be well past eight o'clock and although the twilight still lingers outdoors, Papa says, "Lexie darling, time for you to be in bed. Now be a good girl and go. I'm sure Mama will be back soon."

Reluctantly Lexie goes upstairs to her room. For a time, in her anxiety, she just wanders about. As she looks out the window, she can see the sparklers stuck in the lawn across the street spitting up scarlet, lemon, orange, and blue asterisks and flakes at the leaves of the trees. Finally she undresses and gets into bed, lying there awake, uneasy, staring at the lights and shadows playing on the ceiling. But she must at last have fallen asleep, for she is awakened by the sound of hysterical weeping. She gets out of bed and, in her thin summer voile nightgown, barefooted, starts down the staircase.

Halfway down she is stopped by what she sees. By the lamplight coming from the living room, Mama is visible, stretched out on the floor of the hallway, dragging herself along by her arms and elbows like a wounded animal. The front door is wide open, and the summer night flickers with fireflies. Mama is wearing her dark-blue crepe dress with white gloves and a hat. But the hat is awry on her head, and the dress is hitched up under her on one side so that the garter straps can be seen fastened to the top of the stocking. Near the door lies a small traveling case. Mama is weeping and sobbing wildly, while Papa looks on bewildered. Those two actors are so wrapped up in their tense drama that they don't even see little Lexie standing there on the staircase. How young they seem to Alexandra now! But of course! Mama is only thirty-two, and Papa is twenty-eight. They are both so youthfully vulnerable. Their skin seems so fine and fragile as to be no protection whatsoever. Their faces are thin, pale, drawn. Papa's curly black hair and huge hooked nose stand out sharply against the lamplight from the living room.

At last Papa finds his voice. "Nellie! What is it, Nellie? Why weren't you at home? Where were you? What's the trouble? Tell me! What's happened?"

Mama doesn't reply. He goes over to her and bends down to try to lift her to her feet. But on one knee, Mama pushes him away. She stops her hysterical weeping and glares at Papa with hatred. "You drove him away! You impossible man! Why did you do it?"

Papa frowns down at her, and then says quietly, "Nellie, you're not making sense. I don't know what you're talking about."

"I went to his hotel. He's gone. He went away without leaving any word for me. And no address. He wouldn't do that unless you forced him to. You must have threatened him and bullied him."

Papa stands there for a moment, his mouth open in perplexity. "Who, Nellie? Who are you talking about?"

"Alan!"

"Alan?"

"Yes, Alan Rossiter! Don't pretend! You know very well!"

Papa shakes his head. "No, Nellie, I'm not pretending. I don't know any Alan Rossiter."

But Mama goes on as if she hasn't heard. "You drove him away! He's too much of a gentleman to make a vulgar scene. You counted on that, didn't you? He went away to save my fair name. And he never even got my letters." She begins to weep again, not hysterically as before, but quietly and bitterly. "You drove him away! It was my only chance for happiness in this life! And you drove him away!"

Papa bends down, raises Mama to her feet, and leads her, weeping, to a chair in the living room. Lexie tiptoes down the stairs and stands now in the hallway, still not noticed. What strikes her is Papa's gentleness as he says, "Nellie, you're making a mistake. I don't know any Alan Rossiter." Then he adds, "Come, Nellie, you're all upset. Come, wash up, and I'll get you something to eat. You'll feel better soon. I want you to know I'm glad you're back home with me and the children."

"Back home! Home!" Mama cries mockingly.

"Yes, home. What else but home? Our home and our house."

"*Our* house!"

"Sure our house, Nellie. What else?"

Mama laughs wildly. "A lot you know!"

"What do you mean?"

"I sold the house."

Papa stands there silent while the clock on the mantelpiece ticks loudly away. Finally he says, "I don't believe you. You couldn't do that. I don't believe you." Then, as she says nothing, "You sold the house, Nellie? How could you do that?"

"Oh, there was no trouble about it. The deed was always in my name. Alan managed it all for me."

"But Nellie, how could you do that to me?

And to the children?"

"Don't worry!" says Mama with scorn. "You won't lose a penny by it. You'll be *rich!* He's a good man. And he's a smart man. He's going to make our fortune."

"Who, Nellie? Who's going to make our fortune?"

"Alan Rossiter. I gave him the money from the house to invest. And our savings in the bank too. It was the opportunity of a lifetime. He'll make our fortune. We're going to be fabulously rich!"

For a long time Papa looks at Mama with pity in his eyes, and then he shakes his head slowly. "*Ai,* Nellie, Nellie, *du bist a narrische veib.*"

At that, Mama gets up and goes to the sideboard in the dining room. She is still wearing her white gloves, and her hat is still awry on her head, so that she looks slightly drunk. From the back of a drawer, she takes out the sheaf of parchmentlike papers that Alexandra now holds in her lap. Mama returns to the living room and hands them with triumph to Papa. "There you are! Now you'll believe me! Six thousand shares!

They're going to be worth a hundred thousand dollars in no time at all!"

Papa takes the stock, examines it for a minute or two, and smiles bitterly. "Nellie, this isn't worth the paper it's printed on."

"It's a gold mine."

"All the gold in that mine is right here on this paper."

Mama demands with disdain, "What do *you* know about stocks?"

Papa sighs. "Nellie, Nellie, how could you do this to me? Just think how long it took us to get our house. Think of all the work we put into it. And our savings in the bank. How could you let him cheat you out of it all?"

"Cheat!" Mama says indignantly. "Alan Rossiter is an honorable man."

"Some honorable man! Taking advantage of a foolish woman. *Ai, ich hobb a narr fur a veib.*"

Papa tries to give the stock back to Mama, but she says, "No, that's all for you. I wasn't going to take that with me. I was going to leave everything for you and the children. I didn't want anything from you. Only to go away with

Alan and start a new life."

"Nellie, Nellie, don't you see your Mr. Rossiter was only out to get our money?"

"What does he need with our piddling little money? He's a well-to-do man. You should see the car he drives. And his clothes. He's a real gentleman."

The look Papa gives Mama is full of compassion, almost as though he were gazing at a child. Perhaps this is what Mama was never able to forgive Papa. Perhaps he would have done better to rage and to beat her. Perhaps he failed to understand the *mystère* of the feminine heart. Instead, Papa says, "Nellie, I need you. You know that. I need you to take care of my children. What will Lexie and Teena do without a mother? And who will take care of my Zooneleh? Come, Nellie, you're my *wife*."

"Don't be so sure of that!"

And Mama takes off the wedding band and flings it at Papa, who stands there without moving. The ring falls to the floor, rolls a few feet, and comes to rest against the leg of a chair. At that instant, little Lexie darts into the living room, picks up the ring, and slips it on her finger, clutching it in her fist. For a long time, Papa and Mama, still enveloped in the cocoon of their nightmarish scene, stare uncomprehendingly at this apparition, this little intruder, barefooted and in the thin summer nightgown. Then at last the spell is broken, and Papa walks over to Lexie.

"Lexie darling, give that to me."

Reluctantly, little Lexie unfolds her fist and allows Papa to remove the wedding band. Then Papa goes over to Mama. "Here, Nellie. Let me have your hand."

As if under hypnosis, Mama holds out her hand. Papa slips the wedding band back on her finger. "Come, Nellie," he says. "You better get to bed. I'm sure you'll feel all right in the morning." And he leads her, walking in a trance, slowly up the staircase.

# Epilogue

Last Thursday morning, just as I was lighting the memorial candle on the first anniversary of Mama's death, the long-absent sun broke out of the clouds and streamed through the window curtains into my living room. I had bought the candle in Cleveland, a *yuhrzeit* candle, one of those contained in a squat glass vessel sacramentally inscribed in Hebrew characters. It was now standing on the stone mantel of my fireplace, where the seven-branched candelabrum, the *shtossel,* and the mezuzah are ranged like josses. These reliques of Bubbeh's I had found some years ago, when I happened to be cleaning the top shelf of Mama's kitchen cupboard. Mama had only too readily let me have them. I had polished them piously, and set them on the mantel to be my lares and penates, and to remind me of my heritage.

As the wick caught the flame and I smelled the sanctified beeswax, I remembered that I had put up the coffeepot to boil. I went out into the kitchen and poured a cup of black coffee for myself. I returned to the living room and relaxed in my armchair in front of the fireplace. While I sipped the good hot full-bodied coffee, I gazed at the little flame of remembrance in the *yuhrzeit* candle, ethereal blue in the morning light, and pulsating like a living thing as it inhaled oxygen. And, as might be expected, my thoughts (or, rather, *afterthoughts*) took me back to Mama. And to Papa.

In a way, omitting the bitterness, Aldous was right about Papa. He *was* just a big animal, existing in what the medieval theologian called the order of nature. He just lived contentedly and happily with his body in utter bodiness. All the rest would have seemed to him an efflorescence of hocus-pocus, *bubbeh-meissehs,* old wives' tales. And yet the medieval theologian rightly understood two other orders. There *is* also the order of the mind. And there *is* also the order of the heart. Papa, as we see, *did* have a heart.

Yes, I know. The mind is a meaningless abstraction. And the heart is only a pump with some odd-shaped chambers and some crude valves. But nevertheless! It's what Hamlet refers to. What a piece of work is a man! For out of his bodiness, with its bones and hinges, its muscles and connective tissues, its tubes and pipes and sacks, its bellows and secretors and pumps, its rheums and lymphs and gases, its bubblings and blobbings and belchings and burblings, rises that glorious Acropolis where in the warm sunlight stands the Parthenon of man's thought and man's imagination, and roundabout bloom the flowers of man's compassion and man's charity. Of course, if I'm going to be pedantic, the fact is the Acropolis is just a bare, exposed rock with no flowers whatsoever on it. However, I see a cherub that sees them!

Just think. In all that business with Alan Rossiter, Papa *did* have a heart. I wonder if Mama understood. But how stupid of me! No, much worse than stupid! The unforgivable sin! In the words of my notorious co-religionist, had not Mama hands, organs, dimensions, senses, affections, passions? And if you touched her, did

she not perceive and cogitate, tingle and palpi-
tate? Of course Mama must have understood!
Poor darling foolish Mama! Reduced to a memorial candle and whatever is there in her
grave. Now the ties are dissolved, the liabilities
liquidated, the tablets of the mind wiped clean.
But in the living world, head and heart would
not let go. Here at last our metaphysical poet
can discover the real meaning of the wedding
band. It is the infinite circle of commitment, the
human condition that must endlessly obtain.

I meditatively rotated Mama's wedding
band on my finger. Oh, the human condition!
It's not so much a matter of those vast empty
spaces that frightened Pascal. Nor is it even the
meaningless disasters, the diseases striking without regard to merit of suffering, the idiotic wars
and the famines, the murders and the inhuman
crimes. No, it's the human involvement, the
tears, the broken hearts, the unhinged minds,
the anguished cries. It would be kinder to God
to believe he doesn't exist. No wonder it became
necessary to invent the order of the heart. For
there must be charity. As King Lear learned.
Poor naked wretches, wheresoe'er you are.

But just to be practical. What does Divine Providence provide for man? What is there in it for *him?* Courage. Resolution. Fortitude. Stubbornly doing what he has to do. Obdurately rising above.

All right for those who would fardels bear? Exactly. Courage for its own sake. Resolution for its own sake. Fortitude for its own sake. Even as it confronts and knows. *There* is the triumph of that freak aggregation of over-developed amino acids y-clept man. We need touchstones of human behavior, like Matthew Arnold's touchstones of poetry. By such a touch-stone, Mama was gold. Not twenty-four-carat. Who *is?* But gold enough to pass. Throughout the terrible days and nights with Bubbeh, throughout the unhappy years with Papa, throughout the cruel bleakness after Alan Rossiter, she had the human gift for endurance, for going on.

My coffee cup was empty, and I set it down on the hearth. The bright October sun drew me to the window. I parted the curtains and looked out into the back yard. The week of

steady rain had left its mark. Underfoot, everything was soggy and squishy. Overhead, the
gold-and-crimson pavilion was all in dirty brown
tatters. Not far from the house, I saw a cardinal,
a blue jay, and a dozen chunky black-and-purple
starlings, each busily at the day's work of eating
nearly its weight in seed and bugs. And then,
since Divine Providence does provide sermons
and allegories, I noticed, far off in one corner
of the yard, eight-year-old Christopher Martin
going through some strange contortions, and
so absorbed in what he was doing that he wasn't
aware of me. He would clutch his belly or his
chest or his groin with both hands, grimace
grotesquely as if in unbearable pain, fall to the
ground in a twisted heap, jerk and twitch a few
times, and then lie absolutely still for a minute
or two. Then he would get up and go through it
all again.

Finally I pulled up the window and called,
"Christopher!" I had to call again. "Christopher!"

He looked around at me, startled by my
intrusion.

"Christopher, whatever in the world are you doing?"

"I'm practicing dying."

"Oh," I said. "Well, that's not a bad idea. It'll come in handy one of these days."

# SAMUEL YELLEN

who was born in Lithuania in 1906, was brought to this country as a child. He attended Central High School in Cleveland, Ohio. In 1926 he received his B.A. degree from Western Reserve University, and in 1932 his M.A. degree from Oberlin College. He is now a professor of English at Indiana University, where he has been teaching since 1929. Mr. Yellen, whose short story, "Reginald Pomfret Skelton," was included in *The Best American Short Stories of 1956,* has contributed stories, sketches and poems to *The Atlantic Monthly, The New Yorker, Commentary, The Nation, The Antioch Review, The Yale Review, The New Mexico Quarterly* and other periodicals. He has published *In the House and Out, and Other Poems,* 1952, and *The Passionate Shepherd: A Book of Stories,* 1957. Mr. Yellen and his wife live in Bloomington, Indiana.